TRUST IN ME

Rosie Farnham has battled poverty for years to keep the family's manor and estate running. But faced with the prospect of being thrown out of the home she loves by a handsome stranger, she refuses to budge. Despite the fact that Theo Bradley is entitled to demand vacant possession, she will not leave her home. However, Theo moves in with Rosie *in situ*, which brings another problem to deal with — that of her growing attraction to him.

SUZANNA ROSS

◆

TRUST IN ME

Complete and Unabridged

LINFORD
Leicester

First published in Great Britain in 2012

First Linford Edition
published 2013

A catalogue record for this book is available
from the British Library.

ISBN 978–1–4448–1615–0

Published by
F. A. Thorpe (Publishing)
Anstey, Leicestershire

Set by Words & Graphics Ltd.
Anstey, Leicestershire
Printed and bound in Great Britain by
T. J. International Ltd., Padstow, Cornwall

This book is printed on acid-free paper

1

Evie bounced further into the estate office, blonde hair flying. Can I use the computer?'

At the sound of her sister's voice, Rosie Farnham looked up from the spreadsheet she was working on and sighed.

'Not now, Evie. I'm busy.'

'But I really need to get online.'

What was it with teenagers and technology these days? When Rosie herself had been fifteen, hardly anyone had used a home computer and they'd all managed to amuse themselves just fine. Her sister, on the other hand, couldn't go five minutes without checking Facebook or sending an email.

'Don't you have homework?' she challenged.

Evie smiled triumphantly and played her winning hand. 'Yes, but I need the computer. I have a project I need to research.'

Normally, Rosie would have relented and stepped aside, finished her accounts later. Even if the ancient computer was intended for business use, Evie's school-work always took priority. But this time was different.

'I'm sorry, you're going to have to wait. I have to finish this — it's important.'

Evie folded her slender frame into a chair beside the old desk. 'I need my own computer, really. If I had a laptop I could work in my room without having to bother you.'

'That's not possible at the moment.'

'Don't tell me.' Evie rolled her eyes. 'We've no money.'

Rosie was aware her sister had heard that particular song so many times she must know the lyrics by heart, but Evie could have no concept of just how difficult their circumstances were. She had the intelligence to handle the truth, but there was enough going on in her young life with study and exams. The burden of the estate finances was the last thing Evie needed.

'I'll see what I can do for your birthday,' Rosie promised, although goodness only knew where she would find the money. Perhaps she should speak to Harry. If he knew how crucial a computer of her own was to Evie's studies, maybe he'd leave the estate funds alone this month.

Nah, that wasn't going to work. If the situation hadn't been so serious she'd have burst out laughing at her own ludicrous optimism. Harry would never consider something so selfless.

'How long will you be?' Leaning forward, blonde hair cascading over her face, Evie began to drum her fingers on the desk. 'Ten minutes? Twenty?'

'Look, Evie, I don't know when I'll be finished. And the longer you stay here and complain, the longer it will take me.'

'Can I do anything to help?'

Rosie was touched by the offer, but

she really just needed a few minutes' peace. 'You can get out from under my feet for five minutes. Don't you have anything to do at the sanctuary?'

'All done. Louise and a couple of others helped out today so we got finished quickly.'

'Well, why don't you go and get some fresh air?'

'Okay, I can take a hint. I'll take Jessie for a walk.'

'Thank you.' Rosie bit her lip as her sister left the office. Academically, Evie was very able and had her sights set on being a corporate lawyer. But however bright she might be and however helpful her teachers, she needed support from home. And she needed a computer of her own — one that wasn't needed for estate business . . . and didn't keep crashing every five minutes.

Forcing her attention back to the spreadsheet, Rosie's stomach began to churn as she studied the figures on the ancient screen. There was no hiding the fact she was in serious trouble. Despite operating a huge working overdraft, the estate wouldn't be able to meet its wages obligation this month.

Desperately she moved the cursor down the row of figures, looking for anything that might offer a small glimmer of hope.

'How did it all get into such a mess, Dad?' The question was rhetorical. She knew exactly how this had happened. None of it was her fault. And her father had been dead for five years.

It was no coincidence that five years was exactly the length of time Rosie had faced dire financial problems.

Since her father's demise she'd struggled to keep things together, but it was proving an impossible task. The 'b' word hovered ominously in her thoughts — bankruptcy. She'd refused to consider it, not only because she didn't want to admit defeat, but also because it would mean losing the estate, leaving herself and Evie homeless. But, if things carried on like this, she might not have much choice.

She glanced up helplessly at the large framed poster hanging above her desk in the estate office. Her dad was glaring angrily at the camera, the rest of the band looking equally cross behind him. All part of the image. At the time this had been taken, the band had been doing rather well — they were the angry rockers of their generation and attitude had been all.

She turned her attention back to the spreadsheet. Frantically, she scanned the figures again. Nothing had changed.

This was desperate. People depended on her. She needed a miracle by the end of the month. Even a tiny one would do.

She was praying for inspiration when a knock sounded at the door. A young farmhand popped his head into the untidy office.

'Yes, George?' Distracted by money worries, she was brusque to the point of rudeness and George winced visibly. She immediately regretted her harsh tone and tried to soften the blow by offering an apologetic smile.

George's answering smile was hesitant. 'Sorry to interrupt, Rosie. Ran into a man wandering about the place. He said he was here to see you, so I've brought him up to the house. He's waiting in the sitting room.'

Rosie's eyes narrowed speculatively. She wasn't expecting anyone. 'What man?'

'Said his name's Theo Bradley. Looks official — he's wearing a suit.' George frowned as he took in Rosie's expression. 'Should I have sent him away?'

This was all she needed. She sighed loudly and pushed back from the desk in her swivel chair. It didn't sound good. Rosie didn't get many visits — particularly not from men wearing suits. This man had to be from the bank! She shuddered. The bank had taken to ringing at all times of the day and night, looking to schedule repayment of the estate's overdraft. If she'd had any spare, she would have put money on this man being here in person to demand settlement.

She toyed with the idea of telling George to send the man away. But she was astute enough to realise that if she refused to see him, he'd only come back another day.

'No, that's fine, thank you. I'll be in to see him in a minute.'

Things had been desperate before; perhaps not quite this desperate, but she'd always managed something. For Evie, their staff and tenants she would manage something again this time.

Rosie sat for a few moments and prepared herself. This was going to be unpleasant, no doubt about it — but it had to be done. Head up, shoulders back, she pulled herself up to her full five feet and three inches, tossed her wild red hair away from her face and headed for the door. She might not be in a position to give this debt collector any money, but she was certainly capable of giving him plenty of attitude.

In that respect, at least, there was no doubt she was her father's daughter.

Theo Bradley's displeasure was clearly visible in his frown as he prowled the shabby reception room where he'd been told to wait. From the potholes in the driveway to the unkempt farmhand who'd shown him into the house, this whole situation gave him an enormous sense of foreboding.

This crumbling Grade One medieval pile of stones would need serious attention if there was to be any hope of transforming it into the luxurious get-away his exclusive clientele demanded.

He shook his head. The project was unthinkable — even before taking into account the spinster sisters who were currently in situ. Besides, it was barely a twenty-minute drive from here to Chudley House Hotel — the flagship of the hotel arm of Theo's empire. Despite Lysander's foolish eagerness, Farnham Manor was less than useless as a site for a new hotel.

Theo knew he should never have

come here today, but the temptation to see for himself the evidence of Lysander's lack of judgment had been too much. Until recently, he would have been too engrossed in work to have even bothered with such a diversion — he would have sent an advisor instead. But something had been missing from his life in the past few months. Work was no longer an all-consuming obsession — he was ripe for a new challenge. Sadly, the manor wasn't it.

Glancing at his watch, he wondered how much longer Miss Farnham would be. Even allowing for an elderly lady's prerogative, she'd kept him waiting far longer than politeness allowed. He needed to get away — the sense of decay hovering about the Manor had begun to seriously affect him.

Walking over to the window, he reached out for the catch — the room was unbearably stuffy and musty and . . . He gave a start as the latch came away in his hand.

Theo frowned again as he took in the sorry state of the place. From the damp visible under the peeling wallpaper, to the rotting window frames, the place was a disaster. He hadn't been informed of Harry Farnham's plans for his sisters, but there was one certainty: they couldn't stay here while their affairs were put in order, because the place was unfit for human habitation. Theo would suggest they be dispatched to one of the smaller properties on the estate, until their brother's arrangements could be put into practice. Anywhere would be more comfortable for two elderly ladies than this draughty old house.

At last the door opened behind him. He turned, prepared to greet whichever of the elderly Miss Farnhams had deigned to meet him, and the words expired deep in his throat.

Far from the elderly spinster he'd been expecting, the tiny vision of feminine perfection who stood before him was so lovely she had, quite literally, taken his breath away.

Vaguely aware that he should say something, Theo struggled for coherent thought and failed. He stared, beyond doing anything other than absorbing her utter beauty. It was the emotional equivalent of being hit between the eyes with a brick.

The vision walked towards him, slender legs clad in faded blue denim, sea-green eyes maintaining steady contact.

'Mr Bradley?' Her voice dripped icicles and he noticed, as she walked closer, the sparkle of pure hostility in those mesmerising eyes. 'I'm Rosie Farnham. How can I help you?' She tossed back her wild, red curls and placed her hands on her hips in a militant attitude. Her pale, heart-shaped face offered challenge, her full, Cupid's-bow lips pursed in irritation.

His interest was captured. He wondered briefly who she was — a great-niece of the ladies he was here to see, perhaps. He flashed his most brilliant smile, the smile that normally charmed the most hardened of his adversaries. No response at all from Rosie Farnham — he must be losing his touch.

She took one scathing look at his proffered hand. 'Let's not waste time on pleasantries, Mr Bradley — I'm sure we're both far too busy. What do you want?'

'As you wish.' He had no problem with getting straight to the point although oddly getting out of here no longer featured on his list of priorities. 'I understand I'm expected. I'm here to view the property.'

'To view the property?' A crease appeared between her eyebrows and she looked uncomprehendingly up at him. 'I don't understand. You're not from the bank?'

'No, not from the bank,' he confirmed. 'I'm from Bradley International Investments.'

She relaxed visibly, although it was obvious the name meant very little to her. 'I don't care who you are or where you're from, you can't march in here and demand to look around. Farnham Manor isn't open to the public.'

He glanced again at the shabby surroundings. 'I wouldn't imagine for a minute it is.'

She fixed him with those eyes. As a man well accustomed to dealing with a hostile boardroom, he was surprised to find himself unnerved. He cleared his throat.

'I wonder if I might speak to one of Harry Farnham's sisters.'

Her eyes narrowed as she glared at him with barely concealed hostility. 'I am one of Harry's sisters.'

Shock surged through Theo. His idiot of a brother had led him to believe both Harry Farnham's sisters were advanced in years. Rosie couldn't be much more than mid-twenties.

But at least this should make his task a bit easier. He would still extend the offer of the use of one of the smaller properties on the estate, but at least he no longer faced the prospect of trying to persuade two elderly ladies to move from a home they'd occupied for the best part of a century.

2

Rosie should have guessed Harry would have something to do with this. Harry Farnham, doted-on firstborn offspring — and selfish, self-serving older brother, on whose goodwill she and Evie relied for a roof over their heads. Harry had been behind most of the ills that had befallen the estate in recent years.

The very mention of her brother made Rosie boil with rage. She briefly revisited the fantasy where her visitor was from the bank — the scenario was infinitely preferable.

'Mr Bradley, if you could get to the point?' she snapped, her voice shrill even to her own ears.

She had the beginnings of a headache throbbing merrily at the back of her eyes and Theo Bradley made her feel decidedly uneasy. Men in suits were to be distrusted, in her experience.

Besides, she found his large frame very disconcerting and his fallen-angel good looks thoroughly annoyed her. Completely unreasonable; she shouldn't blame him for being tall and handsome, she acknowledged grudgingly. But, she could definitely blame him for being so confident of his own charm.

There he went again, smiling at her as though she should be grateful for the attention. It made her want to grind her teeth.

'Your brother obviously didn't pass on the message that I'd be calling by this afternoon.'

She eyed him suspiciously. 'I'm not following any of this. What's this nonsense about wanting to look around? And what have you got to do with Harry?'

'Harry's sold Farnham Manor and the estate to my company,' Theo imparted crisply, his golden eyes narrowing as Rosie staggered back towards a chair and dropped into it.

As shock statements went, this had to number among the most shattering

17

imaginable. Rosie opened her mouth to reply but only managed a squeak. Unable to keep looking at him, she focused on a large glass vase sitting on a low table next to the chair. When she had time, she must cut some fresh flowers from the wilderness they called a garden, she mused absurdly.

She knew she needed to say something, but it was hard to breathe, let alone speak.

She must have looked awful because Theo strode towards her, sank down, sat back on his heels and took her hands kindly in his. 'You didn't know?'

She shook her head. No, she hadn't known. It had been many months since she'd seen Harry and his phone calls were always focused on his need for Rosie to send him more money. Nothing had been mentioned about selling the estate. Nothing at all. She would have remembered.

Rosie wanted to snatch her hands away, but somehow she found Theo Bradley's touch comforting, his strength reassuring. Through the coldness of her fingers, she relished his warmth.

Her lips parted. 'I . . . I . . . ' Her feeble attempt at a reply made her feel worse. Under normal circumstances, Rosie always had a ready supply of opinions, but this news had completely thrown her. Of all the possibilities she'd imagined through the countless moments of crisis over the past five years, this one had never featured. She averted her gaze from the pity obvious in Theo's far-too-close-for-comfort face and shook her head again.

'I'm sorry you had to find out like this.' His warm breath fanned her face as he spoke and she gave an involuntary shiver. He truly did sound sorry, but Rosie's mood didn't make her receptive to anyone's sympathy or remorse.

She took a shuddering breath — if they had to leave the manor it would break Evie's heart. Whatever she did, she couldn't allow that to happen.

'It's just not fair,' she managed at last.

'Life often isn't.'

She gave him the dirtiest look from her dirty looks repertoire.

'That's not helpful.'

She wanted to be sick. She'd worked every hour she could to keep the estate going — and she'd given up the chance of a life of her own in the process. And Harry, who'd never had a worry in his life, always got the best of everything, with minimal effort.

'I just can't believe it.'

A frown marred his perfect features. 'I assure you it's true.'

Even though she'd always known exactly how selfish Harry could be, she still couldn't accept he would let her down to this extent — especially with Evie on the scene. Despite Rosie having taken over responsibility for her, Evie was still as much Harry's sister as she was Rosie's. And he knew exactly why Evie was so desperate to stay here.

'Can I call someone for you?'

Dazed, Rosie shook her head. She'd taken care of herself for so long that the idea of Theo calling someone to look after her made her recoil.

She looked down to where her hands still rested in his, hers looking ridiculously small and pale by contrast. His thumbs moved in hypnotic circles on her wrists, making her feel ... strange. She looked up and allowed her bemused gaze to linger on his all-too-perfect face — the haughty cheekbones and strong jaw hinted at model looks. The hardness of his very male face was softened by his mesmeric gold eyes, fringed with long, black lashes. His hair was thick and dark and her fingertips tingled at the thought of what it would feel like to touch. Her eyes settled on his full lips — it would be so easy to tilt forward and brush them with her own. She couldn't help wondering what it would feel like to kiss him ...

'What's going on here?' Evie arrived, just in time to stop Rosie embarrassing herself completely in front of this stranger.

Horrified, she forced herself from her daydream, a flush of awareness warming her face. How, in the name of all that was holy, had she let that happen? Rosie had seen at first-hand what happened when people gave into their longings rather than facing up to their responsibilities. And even if she were to be so tempted, the man who had come to evict her and Evie from their home would be at the bottom of her list of suitable playmates.

'Well?' Evie demanded.

Rosie was aware of Theo as he glanced across and acknowledged the teenager with a brief nod. 'My name's Theo Bradley, I'm here to discuss a business matter with Rosie. And you are?'

'Evie Farnham, Rosie's sister.'

Theo gave a short laugh. 'The second Farnham sister,' he muttered, almost to himself. 'And even younger than the first. Well, that figures.'

With every beat of Rosie's heart, the numbness flowing through her veins slowly seeped away to be replaced by red-hot anger. Anger because Harry had done this to her. Anger because everyone expected she'd roll over and comply with the situation. Anger because this great big man thought he could waltz into her home and tell her he'd just bought the roof she'd lived under all her life. Most of all, anger that in the midst of her distress this stranger had sought to offer her comfort by holding her hands so beguilingly.

She snatched them away from him and stood so abruptly that Theo Bradley very nearly toppled backwards. To her complete annoyance, he regained his balance with the grace of an athlete and leapt instantly to his feet.

She risked a glance over at Evie, who was watching the scene with great interest. That was all Rosie needed. Heaven only knew how she was going to explain this to her sister.

'I'll speak to you in a minute,' she

muttered before turning her attention on Theo Bradley, glowering up at him with all the fury she could muster. He had to know she wouldn't be pushed around like this. 'I've had enough. I think you'd better leave.'

'I'm afraid I'm not going anywhere until we've discussed the matter in hand.'

She was aware of Evie listening to every word, watching each action. Rosie couldn't allow herself to lose control in front of her little sister.

'Evie, the computer's free now — why don't you go and get started on the research you needed to do?'

Evie hung back, reluctant to leave, obviously knowing there was something happening and keen to find out what, exactly.

'It can wait.'

'Evie, please.' The warning tone in Rosie's voice was unmistakable. She rarely used it, but when she did, Evie knew it was best not to argue.

Rosie waited until she had left the

room before rounding on her unwel-
come visitor. 'I refuse to discuss
anything with you. This is my home.
You have no business here. Please
leave.'

He gave the most annoying grin,
showing perfect white teeth. 'I don't
think you understand. You can't order
me to leave my own property.'

Arms folded defensively, she cast him
a withering glance.

'I thought I just had.'

'Rosie, ignoring the issue won't make
it go away. Even if I were to leave now,
it wouldn't change the fact that my
company owns the Farnham Estate.
And it would be impossible for me to
write off an asset of this value —
however much I might want to.'

He sounded so reasonable. She knew
what he said made sense. And yet she
couldn't think further than her need to
keep this roof over her sister's head.

'I can't tolerate a stranger strolling in
here and taking over my home,' she
spat.

25

'You must realise the place is falling apart. Quite apart from any other consideration, it really isn't safe for you to live here.'

Her self-control slipped a notch. She could feel it in the quaking of her fingers, as she lightly touched the cold glass of the vase positioned on the low table next to the chair she'd sat in only moments earlier. It would be so easy to pick it up and throw it at him, to watch as the heavy glass fell and splintered on the floor.

As close to the edge as she'd ever been, she knew she had to get him out of here before she lost it completely. She took a deep breath. 'It's my home and you have no right to criticise it.'

Theo felt like a total louse. It was obvious the manor meant more to her than just somewhere to live. But, as he'd tried to explain, he couldn't walk away. It would leave too big a dent in his balance sheet and he'd be left having to explain himself — something he always tried to avoid.

He shrugged helplessly. 'I can't undo what's been done.'

'My sister and I won't leave our home.' She enunciated with precision. 'We'll invoke squatters' rights, if necessary.'

'Then we have a problem.' Theo held her gaze; her green eyes were practically fizzing and he wondered how such a tiny package of womanhood could contain so much intensity.

'I'll speak to Harry. He'll give you your money back.'

Theo shook his head. He wasn't going to be the one to tell her — he'd passed on enough bad news for one day — but he happened to know that getting the money back from Harry Farnham would be impossible.

'I'm afraid that's not an option,' he said calmly. 'The contracts have been signed.'

She paled visibly. 'You might legally own the manor, but we won't leave. We can't.' Her eyes were bright with unshed tears.

He ran a careless hand through his hair. 'There are empty properties on the estate. How about you and your sister move into one of those, until you can make other arrangements?'

She shook her head. 'That's not going to happen. Evie would be distraught if we had to leave. We stay here at the manor.'

This couldn't be happening. In a minute she'd wake up in her own bed and find Theo Bradley had been nothing more than a cruel figment of her imagination. She'd been overworking and her tiredness, combined with eating too much cheese, had resulted in her subconscious conjuring up her worst nightmare. In the meantime, until she woke, she'd argue her case.

'How do I know you're telling me the truth anyway?' She threw the question out and thought she might have gone too far. Theo Bradley didn't look happy that she was calling his word into question. But she'd made the accusation now, and she pushed the point further. 'For all I know you could be some conman or madman who's taken some insane fancy to my home.'

His breath was released in a loud hiss. 'I can understand your reaction — you're in shock. But I'm not the person you should be angry with, Rosie. You have to face the fact that your brother sold you out.'

'Please go. I really don't want to have to ask you again.'

'Fine.' He reached into the inside pocket of his tailored grey jacket. 'I'll leave you these papers. When you've a mind to read them you'll see they prove every word I've told you is true.' He dropped an envelope onto the table beside the vase. He gave a brief nod and headed for the door. His hand lingered on the handle and then he turned, his golden eyes meeting hers.

'I'll be back soon.'

It sounded like a promise rather than a threat, and Rosie was horrified to realise that she didn't at all mind the prospect of seeing him again. It was only the fact that he was trying to evict her which she objected to.

★   ★   ★

The sunshine was warm as it hit Theo's face — a stark contrast to the arctic reception he'd received from the lovely Miss Rosie Farnham. He hadn't anticipated such a complication — how could he have? No normal person would sell the family home without informing its occupants. It seemed Harry Farnham deserved his reputation as a coward and a lowlife.

But, despite his irritation with the situation in general, he recognised Rosie had been quite magnificent in the way she'd argued her case, even though she must have known it was hopeless. He admired how she'd challenged him, despite the fact that Farnham Manor, in its current state, was hardly worth fighting over.

He couldn't in his wildest imaginings picture Gina disagreeing with him so openly — but then Gina's ways of undermining him had been much more personal. He grimaced as he briefly recalled the disaster zone that had been his last relationship. All his own fault — he should have told her it was over as soon as she'd began to hint about a wedding ring. Well, he'd definitely learned his lesson — never again would he allow any woman to expect more than he was able to give.

Those dark thoughts were quickly surpassed, though, as the memory of a pair of glowing, angry sea-green eyes nudged back into his thoughts. Rosie really was extraordinarily pretty.

As he drove away, he found himself wondering whether she was spoken for.

3

How typical of Rosie's luck — tall, dark and handsome had come knocking on her door and brought a whole load of trouble with him. No surprises there, she supposed — men had always brought trouble to Farnham Manor. Her father, her brother — each a man who'd proved to be far more grief than he was worth.

And now, to top them all, the master troublemaker — tycoon Theo Bradley.

Rosie snatched up the papers he'd left and flicked impatiently through them. She'd have the estate lawyers check them out, but at first glance they seemed to be in order.

Of course they did. She'd never doubted him, not really. He exuded such cool, calm control and utter confidence that Rosie hadn't truly suspected for an instant that he wasn't genuine.

Evie was furiously typing away on the computer when Rosie joined her in the office. She barely looked up from the screen.

Rosie shook her head as she spotted a familiar grey head peering over her sister's shoulder. She sighed. 'Oh, Evie. What have I told you about bringing Jessie into the house?'

Evie shrugged. 'She followed me in. What could I do?'

Rosie sighed, only grateful that her sister hadn't treated their uninvited guest to a visit from the little donkey.

'You could have made sure she was left securely at the sanctuary with the others, that's what.'

Rosie softened as Jessie looked across at her with curious eyes, head to one side. She reached out to stroke the soft, grey ears and couldn't help smiling, despite her problems.

Evie fixed Rosie with a perceptive gaze. 'He was pretty hot — for an old guy.'

Rosie feigned ignorance. 'Who was hot?'

She left Jessie and busied herself with tidying up, putting files and folders back on shelves, shuffling bits of paper into neat piles. Anything so she didn't have to look at her sister.

'That guy, the one who was here just now — Theo Bradley.'

'Was he?' She shrugged a slender shoulder. 'Didn't notice.'

Evie laughed. 'Liar — you couldn't take your eyes off him.'

Sometimes Rosie was exasperated by just how perceptive her sister could be.

'That's because he was a visitor and I was speaking to him.'

'And he couldn't take his eyes off you.'

'That's because he was speaking to me. It's good manners to maintain eye contact with a person when you talk to them. I've told you that often enough.'

'You don't normally look as though you're going to throw yourself at the people you're talking to.' Evie had warmed to her theme and it took all Rosie's efforts to keep calm and not show how much Evie's interrogation was rattling her. 'It looked to me as though you were about to kiss him when I walked in.'

'Oh for heaven's sake.' Rosie slammed a bundle of receipts into a drawer. 'You shouldn't be thinking of a career in law — you should be writing fiction.'

'I know what I saw.' Her sister smirked.

'Then maybe I should take you to get glasses.'

Evie didn't look convinced. 'What did he want?'

The change in direction threw her momentarily. Jessie, fed up of being ignored, left Evie's side and came over to Rosie — obviously thinking she stood more chance of some attention. Glad of the diversion, Rosie took full advantage and patted the animal as she spoke.

'Er, something to do with Harry.' She saw Evie frown and rushed to reassure her. 'Nothing to worry about, I'll sort it out.'

Evie nodded and glanced back at the computer screen.

'Oh-my-gosh!' The expression was shrieked at such volume that Rosie was tempted to cover her ears. 'Just look at this!'

Rosie walked around the desk, with Jessie patiently following, and peered over Evie's shoulder so that she could see the screen and the source of the excitement. She frowned when an image of Theo Bradley stared back.

'You shouldn't Google people, it's intrusive.'

'It's research. Everyone does it. But look, he's mega.'

'Evie, I'm not comfortable with . . . '

'The man's off-the-scale successful. He's thirty-three and a self-made multi-millionaire. Has interests all over the place — including the chain of hotels that owns Chudley House.' Evie mentioned the upmarket hotel, only a short drive away, where the seriously wealthy gathered to relax. 'Look, there's even a photo of him with his helicopter!'

'That's got nothing to do with us, Evie. And I'm not happy with you snooping on him like this.'

'He's not married,' Evie confirmed before looking up to fix her sister with an icy-blue stare. 'You really should have snogged him while you had the chance. He didn't look as though he'd have pushed you away.'

'I don't 'snog' people I don't know.'

'As far as I'm aware, you don't 'snog' anyone — ever. But perhaps you should. You need to find a man. It's not good for you to be on your own.'

Rosie felt the warmth of a guilty blush on her cheeks. If only the thought of kissing Theo Bradley hadn't occurred to her, she might be in a stronger position to fend off Evie's ramblings.

'I don't want a man. Besides, I'm not on my own. I have you.'

'I won't be here forever. When I leave for uni you'll be here by yourself. If I knew you had someone to share the running of the estate with, I'd be much happier.'

Flustered, Rosie tidied pens and paperclips from the desk — anything was better than meeting her sister's perceptive gaze. 'It's kind of you to be worried, but that's not a good reason for me to become involved in a relationship.'

'You could do far worse than Theo. He's gorgeous and rich.'

Shocked, Rosie stared at her sister. Had she really done such a bad job of raising Evie that she was so cynical at fifteen?

'That's a very superficial way to look at it. Relationships are about caring for and loving someone,' she chided. 'Not about going out with someone because they're rich and good-looking.'

'Don't you think you could care for Theo Bradley?' Evie had given up all pretence of working at the computer now.

Could she care about a man like Theo Bradley? The question was ludicrous — their brief acquaintance wasn't based on caring, it was based on his demand for vacant possession.

'Evie — you can stop being silly about this right now.'

'Well, I think you'd make a great couple.' Evie sat back in her chair, a satisfied grin on her face.

Time to put a stop to this. Rosie sniffed loudly. 'When I want your advice about my love life, I'll ask for it. Now it's time you took Jessie back to the sanctuary. And don't bring her into the house again.'

It took a while to persuade Evie to lead the little grey donkey back to her furry friends, but eventually — reluctantly — she complied with Rosie's request.

'And when you get back, can you make a start on dinner, please?' she called after Evie's retreating back.

As soon as Evie was out of earshot, she reached for the phone. The moment she'd simultaneously itched for and dreaded since Theo Bradley dropped

39

his bombshell. Time to call her brother. Her hand hovered over the receiver while she thought over what she should say.

However much she didn't want to make this call, she needed to speak to Harry and sort this out. If not for herself, then for the other estate inhabitants. What if Theo planned to evict the tenants, as he was trying to do with her and Evie? They'd been dependent so long that she didn't think they'd manage in the real world.

She dithered so long that, by the time she'd summoned the courage to dial, Evie was calling to say dinner was ready. Wearily, Rosie got up and made her way to the kitchen. Talking to Harry would have to wait until later.

'We don't have much food in,' Evie complained as she passed over a bowl of tinned chicken soup and some bread.

Rosie made some mental calculations. 'I'll go shopping next week,' she decided. Until then they'd have to live off whatever was there. 'Now, did you take Jessie back to the sanctuary?'

Evie nodded.

'Good. How's Mr Kennedy?'

Evie smiled, pleased for the chance to talk about her newest animal. 'Fine. He seems happy. He was pleased to see Jessie — trotted up to the gate to meet us. I think he'd missed her, even though she'd only been out of the field for half an hour or so.'

Rosie was pleased with the news. Mr Kennedy had spent much of the past ten years as an only donkey — a pet to a family with three children — and he hadn't seen one of his own kind in all that time. With the children all grown up, the family had been keen to make alternative arrangements. Evie had been delighted to offer him a home.

Rosie smiled as she recalled how the other donkeys had gathered around to watch as he'd trotted off the trailer and rolled in the warm grass. Then he'd immediately trotted off around the field with the group. But, even while he was in his element as part of the group, it was little Jessie whom he followed with utter devotion.

'It might be an idea to bring him out with you, if you take Jessie for a walk in future. He seems to have formed a bit of an attachment and we don't want him pining. But make sure you put a halter on him — just until we find out what he's about.'

* * *

After they'd eaten, Rosie was empowered with renewed determination to make the call to Harry. She went back into the estate office and picked up the phone, her hand trembling as she punched in the number. Able to think rationally at last, she reasoned that there had to be some mistake. Harry couldn't have sold the manor and left Evie and herself homeless. He might not be the most caring brother in the world, but surely he wouldn't be so heartless?

As she waited for him to answer the

call, she remembered Harry's outright fury five years ago when he'd discovered the terms of his inheritance. He'd been left the estate, the manor, everything — but all to be held in trust until he turned forty.

Harry's fortieth birthday had been last month.

A sliver of doubt entered her mind, nudged a little . . . and, in the space of a second, she recognised the truth of the situation: Selling out herself and Evie was exactly what Harry had done.

The answering machine kicked in and she waited for the beep. 'Harry, this is Rosie. I need to talk to you. It's urgent. Call me as soon as you get this message.'

She knew he probably wouldn't bother calling back. Harry didn't like confrontation. He'd avoid her until the dust had settled. But she suspected the anger surging through her, making her head throb merrily, would never abate. Harry would have to run until the end of time because she'd never forgive him for this.

Needing to hear a friendly voice, she dialled her best friend's number. Since Julia had moved to the area and married the local vet, she'd proved to be someone to rely on. And she was the only person Rosie was happy to confide in.

'Harry's done *what?*' Julia was incredulous.

'I didn't think it could be true, either.' Rosie bit her lip. Now she'd spoken about it to Julia, it made it all seem very real. 'But the papers are all in order and it does seem like something Harry might do.'

'But not to tell you . . . ' Julia harrumphed down the line. 'He really is a first class creep, that man.'

'You're not telling me anything I don't already know.'

'How has Evie taken the news?'

'I haven't told her. I don't want her knowing until I've sorted something out.'

'She'd cope, you know.'

'I know. But she's got exams coming up and . . . well, you know why she wants to stay here.'

There was silence down the line and, for a moment, Rosie thought Julia had gone. At last she spoke again. 'There's always a place for you both — here with me, Bob and Louise.'

'Thank you.' This wasn't the first time Julia had made such a generous offer and it was comforting to know that they wouldn't be out on the streets if they could no longer live on the estate. What would she do without such good friends?

Rosie's chat with Julia restored some sense of normality, but as soon as she replaced the receiver her current predicament returned to haunt her with a vengeance.

'Harry's a rotten brother,' she muttered to herself. If he ever bothered to call her back, she'd waste no time in telling him so.

Not for the first time she experienced

a glimmer of fury towards her dead dad. He'd left every last bean to Harry, wanting to keep it all in the Farnham family and expecting that his two daughters would marry and have no need of independent finance. She still found it odd that Mick Farnham had upheld such an unfair, old-fashioned idea, especially considering his own lifestyle.

Rosie shook her head, trying to clear her thoughts. She had to find a solution. Not only did Harry's betrayal leave her homeless, it also left her jobless. The only work experience she had was running the estate . . .

The answer came to her in a blinding flash — she'd have to convince Theo Bradley he needed to keep her on to manage the estate. He hadn't discussed his plans, but judging from his online CV she doubted that he intended to roll up his expensive shirt sleeves and run the place himself. He'd need a manager. And who better than Rosie to apply for the post?

There was only one problem — she and Theo Bradley hadn't exactly hit it off at their first meeting. Looking back, she realised he'd been kind as he'd broken the awful news. But, in return, she'd been horrid. Truly horrid. It wasn't his fault Harry had sold the estate, but, in her brother's absence, she'd blamed him anyway. Why would he want to employ her after that?

She'd have to find some way to charm him.

Oh, no. Not good.

Rosie had no inclination towards natural charm. Besides, she'd been too busy in recent years to entertain thoughts of charming anyone. She didn't believe in dressing things up in fancy words and smiling at people she didn't want to smile at.

But now she had no choice. With Evie in the equation, she couldn't allow their home to be lost. For Evie's sake, Rosie would have to work against a lifetime of conditioning and be nice.

She shuddered in horror at the prospect.

★ ★ ★

'How did it go at the new property, boss?' Andy, Theo's assistant, greeted him as they caught up at Chudley House later in the evening.

Theo smiled as he remembered how he had been thrown off his own property by a spitting, fizzing bundle of fury. 'All in hand,' was all he said. There was no doubt about it, something about Rosie Farnham had got to him.

He knew that if he had any sense, he would instruct his lawyers to deal with the matter and step away. He didn't need to go anywhere near Farnham Manor again. But, from the moment he'd driven away, his mind had been drawn back to the sorry excuse of an estate — and the woman who ran the place.

In truth, Theo had become bored with his life. Everything fell into place with alarming ease and he relished the prospect of getting involved with the estate and working to bring it into some kind of order. Especially as Rosie would be there.

'I'm taking some time off,' he informed Andy. 'So we'd better get down to business because I won't be available starting first thing tomorrow morning.'

Theo was going back to Farnham Manor as soon as possible. He wanted to make sure Rosie was okay — he knew today's news had floored her. But more than that, he wanted an excuse to see her again.

'There's nothing in your diary.' Andy sounded puzzled. 'Is it business?'

Theo smiled to himself. 'Kind of.'

Andy's eyebrows shot up towards his hairline but he wisely offered no comment.

★　★　★

Rosie's exhaustion was clearly etched on her face the next morning. She'd barely slept and, far from enjoying a lazy start on a Saturday, she had been up and ready for work by six — as she was most mornings.

The place was quiet in a way it never was at any other time. She liked it like this. Most of the tenants didn't rise until lunchtime, a habit acquired during their hard rocker days, she imagined. Evie always liked to sleep in at weekends, too — she was always up early each weekday, to see to her donkeys before school, so she deserved a bit of a lie-in.

With a sigh, Rosie went into the office. Having already been over to the sanctuary to check on things, there was no longer room for procrastination. She had to concentrate on the burning issue of their future.

She stifled a yawn. She'd worn herself out during the long hours since she'd seen off Theo Bradley. She'd paced and planned and tried to decide what to do for the best. He had to be the biggest threat to her peace of mind she'd ever encountered, and she'd come to the conclusion that she needed to be the one to make the first move — she couldn't bear the idea of sitting around waiting for him to contact her.

She decided the internet was her best chance. She should be able to find a contact number for him on that website Evie had discovered. She'd barely re-booted the ancient machine for a second time after it crashed, managed to find the details of his vast empire and settled down to read, when the doorbell rang.

Irritated by the interruption, she shoved her chair away from her desk. She couldn't imagine who would be calling at this time on a Saturday, but whoever it was had already annoyed her. Now she'd decided on a course of action, she wanted to make a start on her plan. And from what she'd learned about him so far, she was going to need all her concentration and planning know-how to outwit Theo Bradley. The man was off-the-scale successful, as Evie had said.

But she was hopeful. Once he'd looked over the accounts, he'd see she knew what she was doing. Now that Harry would no longer be able to plunder the estate coffers, they could soon have a thriving concern, with strawberries flourishing in the polytunnels and acres of Christmas tree saplings. And she needed a proper business plan, she decided as she headed out into the hall — she would formulate a business plan and present it in a professional manner. That was her best hope.

The bell rang again in four short bursts. 'Okay, I'm here!' she called impatiently, throwing open the door.

Nothing could have prepared her for the sight that greeted her — six foot four inches of prime manhood, a suitcase at his feet and a challenging gleam in his golden eyes.

'I told you I'd be back,' he announced, and a slow grin spread over his face.

4

The last person she'd expected. Rosie's stomach lurched. After the reception she'd given Theo yesterday, and with the knowledge gleaned from the internet, she had fully expected him to set his lawyers on her rather than return in person.

The intimidating business suit from yesterday had been swapped for casual black jeans and black shirt. The ensemble made him look devastatingly handsome, she grudgingly acknowledged — even more so than she remembered.

Deep, steadying breath. *Remember to be charming*, she reminded herself as she wondered briefly at the significance of the suitcase. She didn't smile — couldn't bring herself to go that far on her charm offensive — but neither did she feel the urge to throw something at him. That had to be progress.

'I was just trying to find your telephone number,' she said.

He quirked a dark eyebrow. 'Really?'

Why had she told him that? In his warped male mind he'd probably concocted a scenario where she was desperately searching for his number to ask him out.

'Purely for business reasons,' she added.

'If you say so.'

He was flirting, there was no other word for it. The urge to throw something returned with a vengeance. Her resolution hadn't lasted long after all. She felt a warm blush spread over her face. 'What other reason would there be?'

He laughed softly and a shiver ran down her spine.

'None at all. Can I come in?'

She stepped aside and he walked past her into the manor. Immediately she felt invaded. He was too big, too close . . . just too much. She showed him into the sitting room and he sat on the sofa. She chose the furthest chair and settled on it.

'Why were you looking for my number?'

As he spoke, she realised with blinding clarity what made his presence in her home so unsettling — the buzz of pure, unadulterated testosterone that filled the air around him.

She couldn't think straight in his presence right now. No way could she put her idea to him while he'd caught her so off balance by calling around unannounced — again. She needed to buy some time, to collect her thoughts and convince herself she found him no more attractive than a broom.

'I wanted to speak to you about the tenants. I'm worried about what will happen to them. They've lived here for years — some of them were even in Dad's band.'

'I have no immediate plans to make any changes to the tenancy agreements.'

She nodded. That was very reassuring and should lead naturally into her asking about his plans for the estate — for employing a manager. But she still couldn't bring herself to say the words.

She blamed Evie. If her sister hadn't started that stupid nonsense about Rosie needing a man, she wouldn't be thinking like this. She conveniently forgot that she'd been wondering what it might be like to run her fingers through his hair, to kiss him, before her sister mentioned anything about Theo being hot.

Remember the plan, she told herself. *Forget he's a man.* Despite this, she suspected she would have been able to appreciate the fact Theo Bradley was a man even in the middle of a nuclear explosion.

Still ignoring his question, she forged ahead with one of her own. 'Why have you brought a suitcase?'

He glanced across at the suitcase he'd carelessly dropped inside the door. 'I'm staying.'

'Staying?' She wrinkled her nose. 'Staying where?'

'Here,' he intoned. 'At the manor. With you.'

'No, I'm sorry. That's not possible.'

His smile would have melted a lesser woman on the spot. 'It's necessary. I need to get to know the inner workings of the estate, and the best way to do that is to stay here.'

'But . . . '

'I'll be finished a lot quicker if I don't have to commute — I can give the estate my undivided attention. Besides, the house is so big I'm sure you won't even notice I'm here.'

Rosie opened and closed her mouth. She wanted to object in the strongest terms, but she realised she probably didn't have a legal leg to stand on. And she didn't want to antagonise him. Not before she had managed to speak to him about the estate.

'I don't know how I'm going to explain this to Evie.'

'I'm sure she'll accept me moving in

as a natural development for the new owner.' She felt her face fall and saw his surprised look as he registered her expression. 'You haven't told her, have you?'

Rosie shook her head. 'I didn't know how. I was hoping . . . well, I don't know what I was hoping for. But it will break Evie's heart to leave.'

'I can understand she's attached to the place, but young people are adaptable. She'll be okay.'

Rosie wanted to scream. 'You don't understand — she's got her donkeys and besides . . . '

'Her *donkeys?*' His eyebrows reached his hairline.

'Well, yes. She's set up a donkey sanctuary on the estate. So far she's rescued four — in addition to her own, Jessie.'

'So let me get this straight.' He shifted forward on the sofa, his expression incredulous. 'You're refusing to move because your sister's taken in a collection of animals?'

'There's more to it than that.' She bit her lip. It was none of his business that Evie wanted to stay here so that her mother could find her. Best not to mention it. 'Those donkeys mean a lot to Evie. Her life hasn't been easy and they've given her something to focus on.'

He was silent for a moment, then his brow creased. 'There's a huge difference in age between you, Evie and your brother.'

She got the feeling that wasn't what Theo had intended to say, but she decided to let it go for now. And it must be confusing — sometimes the age difference between the siblings confused her. Harry was forty, she was thirty-one and Evie was still a schoolgirl.

'Harry, Evie and I all have different mothers,' she explained. 'Dad lived the genuine rock star lifestyle.'

'Your father was Mick Farnham — frontman with The Noise, wasn't he?'

Rosie nodded and settled back into

her chair. 'That was Dad — the original noisy boy.'

'He had quite a reputation in his day.'

Theo had obviously done his homework, but she would have expected nothing less. He hadn't achieved the status of a multi-millionaire by being unprepared.

'I can't deny it. And he lived his life fast and loose until he died five years ago.' Rosie glanced down to where her hands rested on her lap. Normally she guarded against sharing any details about her father's life, but it didn't seem strange to talk to Theo. If he made a habit of being this amenable, then his staying here might not be such a bad idea, she reflected — it would give her more time to persuade him round to her plans.

He sat back against the cushions. 'And now you live here on your own with your sister?'

'Yep, just the two of us.'

'Does Harry visit often?'

Rosie's laugh was humourless. 'You

must be joking. Harry's interest in the estate is limited to how much money he can — could — take out of it.'

'Evie will understand it's not your fault.'

'Perhaps.' She sighed and got to her feet. 'Come on, I'll show you to the spare room. And then I need to talk to you.'

★　★　★

He'd expected an argument — Rosie Farnham in full battle mode had been quite something. It was a surprise that she'd surrendered with such ease. This wasn't the same Rosie who'd thrown him out yesterday. He suspected there might be a hidden agenda to her sudden change in demeanour — she had to be up to something. But at least she looked fairly happy that he was staying, and that had to be progress.

Theo grabbed his suitcase and followed Rosie up the stairs, enjoying the view of her denim-clad bottom as it

61

undulated practically at eye level in front of him.

While Rosie proved to be a growing attraction, by contrast, the more he saw of the Manor the worse it got. He couldn't believe he'd insisted on staying here when the luxury of Chudley House beckoned from less than half an hour's drive away. The squalor and decay of the old building should have made him run a mile, but Rosie Farnham was a mighty temptation.

'The place is falling apart,' he muttered as he stepped over fallen chunks of plaster and cornice littering the landing.

'Sure is,' she replied cheerfully. 'Are you still sure you want to stay?'

He glanced at her quirkily arched eyebrow, the challenging glint in her sea-green eyes and the ruined state of the building faded from prominence in his mind.

'More than ever,' he assured her.

The spare room, thankfully, offered more comfort than he could possibly have expected from what he'd seen of the house — if he could ignore the décor.

'Pink and girlish, I'm afraid.' No hint of an apology in her tone, he noted. 'This is where Evie's friends sleep when they stay over.'

'I can live with it.' He dropped his suitcase onto the cerise carpet at the foot of the bed. He hadn't realised pink came in so many varying shades. Not a problem; Theo was a master of focus and he assured himself he could effectively blank out his surroundings and concentrate on formulating a plan of action. He needed to decide what he was going to do with the place.

His initial reaction, when he'd first realised how useless the estate would be as a hotel, had been to offer it for immediate sale in as tantalising a package as possible. He knew he'd probably make a loss — a combination of the current economic climate and Lysander foolishly agreeing a purchase price way above the market value would see to that. But Theo had deemed writing off a loss more prudent than throwing more money at the place. And finding a buyer shouldn't pose a problem — if the price was right — as there was always someone keen to buy a country retreat and put their own stamp on it. If he was honest, selling was still probably the sensible option.

But something had changed and he didn't feel particularly sensible. The estate meant a great deal to Rosie and he knew if he got rid of it without considering any other possible options, she would be deeply hurt. And that was the last thing he wanted.

As Rosie turned to walk away, he called after her, 'Aren't you going to tell me what you want to talk to me about?'

Rosie made a valiant attempt to draw on all her resources. She needed to make this good — so good he wouldn't be able to refuse her. She wasn't ready to broach the subject, not anywhere near, but she needed to do this now — for Evie's sake. And she'd already evaded the issue once.

'I was thinking . . . ' She took another breath. This was harder than she'd ever imagined it would be — being forced to grovel to the man Harry had sold out to made her feel ill. But, for Evie, she had to at least try. 'You'll need to take on a manager — someone to run the estate day to day . . . '

He glanced at her thoughtfully. 'Are you applying for the job?'

'I am. If you let me show you the books, you'll see that, if Harry's no longer helping himself to the profits, I can really make this work.'

Rosie watched as he ran his hand through his thick black hair. 'I would consider you, of course I would. But I haven't decided what I'm going to do with the place yet.'

Rosie took a minute to digest the news. 'Haven't decided?' she repeated faintly, aware on some level that she sounded like an idiot as her hopes came perilously close to being dashed.

'Not yet. I need to see exactly what's

happening here before I decide what to do.'

This was sounding as though her precious home was just another business deal. Which to him, of course, was exactly what it did represent.

She closed her eyes briefly before she dared to ask, 'What plans are you considering?' She remembered his property interests and felt as though she might faint as a nightmare scenario began to unfold in glorious Technicolor in her mind. 'What are you going to do to the estate? Break it up into tiny pieces so that some property developers can build as many houses as they can cram in?'

Ah, there was his hissing, spitting sparring partner.

Her face had turned the same deep pink as the bedcover and he felt a momentary pang of guilt — she hadn't had the easiest time of it since he'd broken the news, and now he was making things worse.

It went completely against type, but

he felt an overwhelming urge to quell this tiny redhead's fear. He decided to abandon his usual policy of never explaining himself.

'I own a chain of luxury country hotels,' he told her quietly. He scrutinised her face keenly, looking for some change in her expression, but she continued to stare at him with open hostility.

'I know that — I've done my homework. Evie Googled you and we read your online biography. I know all about the hotels, the steel and the construction interests. I also know that business rivals quake in your presence — but I'm not a business rival and I'm not scared of you.'

'I don't want you to be scared of me, Rosie.' That was part of the attraction — the fact that she stood up to him without hesitation. And, rather than being offended by the intrusion, he approved of the fact the sisters had researched him. 'When I first heard the company had acquired the manor, it briefly crossed my mind it might do as a site for another hotel.'

'You want to turn the manor into some sort of glorified bed and break-fast? But you can't possibly . . . '

'I was thinking more a luxury hotel and spa,' he corrected.

'But there would be people . . . *strangers* . . . staying in my home . . . ' she stammered.

'Your brother sold up. It's no longer your home,' he pointed out reasonably. 'And judging by what I've seen of the state of the place, the buy-out didn't come a minute too soon.'

'But a hotel . . . '

He grimaced. 'Unfortunately, the manor's less than useless as a hotel — too close to Chudley House. So, I could sell. Or . . . '

'Or what?'

'One of the other options might be to renovate and live here myself.' Where had that idea come from, he wondered?

He didn't need a home; had never wanted one in the traditional sense. He had the use of a private luxury suite in every hotel and resort he owned around the world, and that arrangement suited him just fine. Home had never been a haven for Theo, and the very word conjured up particularly unpleasant childhood memories. So why had he suddenly fallen prey to an inexplicable nesting instinct?

It came back to the challenge he'd been missing. Renovating this manor would give him a new focus. And, if he still didn't feel inclined to settle down to a permanent home once the project had been completed, well, he could always sell up at that point.

5

Yet again, he had rendered Rosie speechless. Not only was it very obvious there would be no place for herself and Evie here, she was also left still wondering what would become of the estate's other inhabitants?

She had to convince him the best course of action would be to leave the place as it was. If left to her own devices, she'd be able to run the estate at a profit. She knew it. If only Theo would give her the chance she knew she could make it work.

'The staff . . . ' she croaked. 'The tenants . . . You promised they could stay. You might not feel bad about throwing me and Evie out of the manor, but owning the estate brings responsibilities. Some of the families have farmed estate land for generations. And the tenants in the cottages would never be able to look after themselves.'

'Why not? What's wrong with them?'

'Nothing as such, but they've been here since Dad's days — people he met through the business.'

He shook his head. 'So, as well as a bunch of useless animals, we have a collection of musical has-beens and hangers-on?'

'That's not fair. You can't speak about my tenants like that — they all pay their rent. I'm worried about them, that's all.'

'I realise that. As I said, I'm just throwing ideas out there at the moment. Nothing's been decided yet, but I can tell you nobody will be left homeless — I give you my word.'

'Apart from me and Evie.'

'For what it's worth, I do feel bad about what's happened. But the manor's falling down around your undeniably pretty ears. Even if my foolish brother hadn't squandered company money on it, your days here were numbered. If things are left as they are, it's only a matter of time before the place is condemned as unfit for human habitation. You must see that.'

She winced. She knew he was right, but she wasn't happy that it was Theo who was taking the time to point out the estate's deficiencies. This was her home, and she loved it. She'd put her life and soul into the place from the moment she'd been old enough to realise she had a soul.

Wounded, she glared at him. 'I'm well aware the place could do with . . . a little maintenance.'

'Understatement of the century.'

'Well, if it's so awful, why did you refuse my offer to try to persuade Harry to give you your money back?'

He paused so long that she thought he wouldn't reply. But, eventually, he drew a loud breath and spoke.

'This isn't the time to go into it and I shouldn't be the one to tell you. I've already had to do too much of Harry's dirty work.'

She could keep asking and annoy

him. Or she could accept his answer for now and try to find out, another time, what he meant by it.

His golden eyes fixed on her, and a dark shiver ran through her. Probably best to leave it for now. She stared at him, trying to work out what made him tick. She could see no clues. His dark face remained expressionless, his golden eyes impenetrable.

'You're obviously very attached to the estate. Am I right to assume your family has a history at the manor stretching back as far as some of the tenant farmers' families?'

Even while Rosie seethed quietly, she reminded herself she still couldn't afford to alienate him. She took a deep breath.

'No — actually we've only been here since the seventies.'

Theo frowned. 'Then why are you so against moving out? I wouldn't see you and your sister homeless — you're welcome to one of the estate cottages for as long as you need it. You give the impression you're emotionally attached to the manor.'

'I *am* emotionally attached,' she snapped. 'Our history here might be measured in decades rather than centuries, but we have obligations to the staff and tenants. Evie and I were both born here, we've lived here all our lives. My mother died in this house. Besides, it was important to Dad. His fame might have been fleeting, but he saw the manor as something he attained by his own efforts. Something he could hand down to future generations — that's why he renamed it after the family.'

Theo's lips quirked. 'Wasn't that a bit narcissistic?'

Rosie smiled despite herself. 'Undoubtedly, but he got away with it. A certain arrogance was expected of a rock star of his generation. Besides,' she couldn't resist sniping, 'I'm sure it's no more narcissistic than naming a company after yourself.'

'Point taken.' He grinned and sat

down on the Barbie-pink bedspread. Infuriatingly, instead of looking ridiculous, the colour merely accentuated his masculinity. 'Why don't you tell me a bit more about your father?'

'I don't talk about him much . . . ' Rosie began with reluctance.

'It might help,' he coaxed gently. 'It can't be easy for you that he left the manor to your brother. You must be carrying a lot of resentment.'

'A red hot alpha male, a big-shot businessman and now an armchair psychologist,' she marvelled with oodles of sarcasm. 'Do you have any other talents I should know about?'

He glanced fleetingly at the bed he was sitting on and horror flooded through her. How could she have forgotten that she was in his bedroom? She decided to beat a hasty retreat.

'We can continue this conversation downstairs after you've unpacked,' she shot over her shoulder.

* * *

Saturday or not, Evie was up and dressed by the time Rosie went back downstairs — she was in the kitchen, pouring cereal into a bowl and adding generous spoonfuls of sugar.

'You'll get worms putting that much sugar on your breakfast.' Rosie quoted the old wives' tale and Evie laughed, scattering a coating of sugar over the work surface in the process.

'That might have worked on me when I was seven, but I happen to know you only get worms by ingesting their eggs.'

Momentarily distracted, Rosie managed a smile. She knew she'd have to warn her sister of their visitor — but where did she start? 'What do you have planned for today?' she asked.

'Going to check on things in the sanctuary first thing, then over to see Louise. Julia's invited me for lunch and said we could take the horses out this afternoon.'

Rosie nodded. She thanked heaven for Julia. This wasn't the first time she'd fed Evie when the manor's pantry was bare. Best to get the news of their visitor out in the open before she went out, though.

'Erm . . . Evie . . . '

'Mmm?' Evie was more interested in spooning cereal into her mouth than listening.

'You know that man who was here yesterday?'

That got her interest. She dropped her spoon into the bowl and grinned. 'The hot guy?'

'Er . . . ' Rosie shifted uncomfortably. 'Yes, I suppose so. The hot guy.'

'What about him?'

'He's going to be staying here with us for a while.'

The smile was instantly wiped off Evie's face and her jaw dropped. Yes, much the reaction Rosie had been expecting — and not too far away from her own when Theo first announced his plan to move in.

'Why?' Evie managed at last.

Rosie took a cloth and wiped sugar

from the worktop. She couldn't meet Evie's eye — and she definitely couldn't tell her sister the entire truth. At any rate, not until she'd caught up with Harry and made some definite plans for the future.

'He wants to look over the estate, to see how it all works,' she muttered, careful to keep to the truth — just not the whole truth. 'And I've agreed it's a good idea.'

'Ooookaaay . . . ' It was obvious Evie suspected something more, but from the way she was smiling it was also very obvious that Evie's suppositions were a good way from the truth.

The door opened and they both looked up expectantly. It was George, in for his break. He sat down beside Evie, and Rosie placed a steaming mug of hot tea on the table in front of him.

'Thanks.' He grinned.

'Rosie's moved a man into the manor!' Evie mischievously broke the news.

George's astonished expression would

have made Rosie laugh out loud, had she not been so mortified.

'It's not how Evie makes it sound,' she insisted, her face flaming. 'He's here to observe the workings of the estate. That's all.' She glared at her sister.

Thankfully, George wasn't the type to spread rumours. He nodded, took a sip of tea and said no more on the subject.

'How are your parents?' Rosie asked. George's parents were a bit of a nightmare — demanding and helpless, they relied on their teenage son far too much.

'Okay,' he replied, although it was obvious from his expression they were anything but. Rosie wished she was the type of person who could comfort another spontaneously — George looked as if he could do with a friendly hug.

She could have cheered when Evie moved closer and draped a supportive arm around him. Her sister was a sweetheart.

The door crashed open again and this time three pairs of eyes turned to look, but instead of Theo, Julia appeared.

'Hey, everybody.' Her smile faded when she saw Evie and George sitting so close together — with Evie's arm around his shoulders. 'What's going on?'

'Nothing.' Evie grinned, sitting back in her chair.

Rosie could see Julia wasn't happy and was surprised by her reaction. It wasn't like her to be so grumpy.

'It's good to see you,' she chipped in, trying to lighten the suddenly uncomfortable atmosphere. 'Can I get you a coffee?'

Julia tucked a strand of her fashionably short blonde hair behind her ear and turned to face Rosie, her brow still furrowed.

'No, thank you. I've only popped by to see if Evie wants to come into town for some shopping with me and Louise, before we have lunch.'

'Yes, please.' Evie didn't hesitate. 'But I'll need to check the sanctuary. I haven't been up there yet today.'

'I have, this morning,' Rosie told her. 'Everything's fine.'

'And Louise is there now,' Julia added. 'When I dropped her off on the way here, two of your volunteers seemed to have everything in hand.'

Never one to turn down a trip into town, Evie was on her feet instantly. And she was so excited at the prospect, she neglected to mention their new lodger, Rosie noted gratefully. Although she was sure her sister would rectify that omission before long.

* * *

Theo caught up with Rosie in the ancient kitchen — the room looked as though it had been badly updated at some time in the sixties and barely touched since. He winced as he sat down at the Formica-topped table, but was quickly distracted by the sight of

81

Rosie on her knees, rummaging in one of the cupboards. She emerged, triumphant with a food can in her hand.

She placed her free hand on her hip and stared up defiantly. 'I can only offer you beans on toast for lunch.'

These days Theo's meals were prepared by the finest chefs at his hotels. He hadn't contemplated eating beans on toast since his impoverished childhood, but suddenly, no meal had ever seemed more tempting. 'Sounds fine to me.'

She dished up with little fuss, putting a plate in front of him and another on the table for herself.

'Your sister isn't joining us?'

Rosie shook her head. 'She's eating at a friend's.'

A blinding flash of intuition warned him she wasn't being awkward in offering him such basic food. It wasn't like him to make such an oversight, especially when it should be obvious to anyone that she was living in a state of abject poverty. He should have been more sensitive to the fact that she would be worried about the extra financial burden an uninvited guest would bring, and he should have immediately put her mind at rest.

'I'll provide the meals from now on,' he told her. 'I don't expect you to pay for my upkeep.'

The fleeting look of relief that crossed her pale face was unmistakable, and the very fact that she didn't argue told him all he needed to know.

They ate in companionable silence and when they were tidying away, Theo opened up the conversation, hoping to coax her into relaxing in his company. 'You were going to tell me about your father?'

She made a production of laying the cutlery back in its drawer, obviously carefully considering her answer.

'Dad was a working class lad made good,' she eventually shared. 'He bought the manor when he was at the height of his fame, but by that time the band was squabbling over rights and royalties. They didn't last at the top as long as they might have done. He married Mum shortly after his band imploded.'

'And your dad settled down to the life of a country gent?'

'Hardly.' Rosie wrinkled her nose. 'Dad wasn't the settling down sort. A wedding ring couldn't curtail his extra-curricular activities, I'm afraid.'

'He had an affair?'

She didn't answer straight away and he thought he'd pushed too far.

'Plural. He had affairs.' Rosie took the plates he handed her, her concentration on stacking them in the cupboard out of proportion to the difficulty of the task. 'Legend has it he went off with one of the bridesmaids half way through the wedding reception. Neither of them was seen for two days.' Rosie gave a short, humourless laugh.

'Why did your mother stay with him?'

Rosie shrugged and slammed the

cupboard door. 'Guess we'll never know. If I'd married a man who did something like that, I'd divorce him before the ink dried on the marriage certificate. That's if I hadn't murdered him first.'

'You didn't get on with your father?'

Rosie thought about the father she had adored. She'd loved him without question — still did — but she'd never understood why he behaved as he had towards his wives and girlfriends.

'Oh, I got on fine with him. But I didn't condone his lifestyle. Even though they didn't always get on, the rest of the band all moved to live on the estate, which didn't help. He had no incentive to be a grown-up while his childhood friends were encouraging him to live on the wild side.'

Why was she revealing so much to this stranger? Why was she confiding things to Theo which she barely acknowledged to herself? Immediately, she stopped talking. She'd said more than enough already and shared more about herself than she'd ever wanted to do. She could feel his eyes on her, and it seemed he could read her mind. And she was furious with him for it.

'What's wrong, Rosie?' he asked softly.

'Nothing.' She stared at him through narrowed eyes.

What had just happened there? She didn't understand it. Theo Bradley had to be in cahoots with the devil — that was the only explanation. How else could he have tempted her to speak so freely?

6

'I know you'll never control that lot who live in the cottages, but I thought you'd put an end to shenanigans up at the manor at least!' Miss Morris, the village shopkeeper, didn't mince her words as she cast a beady eye towards Rosie's uninvited guest.

Rosie was appalled. 'There are no 'shenanigans' at the manor, I can assure you.'

'Hmm.' Miss Morris glanced meaningfully over at Theo again before turning her attention to packing groceries into shopping bags. 'If you say so.'

Rosie could feel her colour rising and glared at Theo with her best look-what-you've-done-now expression firmly in place. Infuriatingly, he didn't seem in the least concerned. Definitely not a gentleman, or he would have backed her up. Instead, as she watched, he shrugged a shoulder and she could have sworn he was suppressing a grin. She grabbed a carrier bag and left the shop with as much dignity as she could muster.

'Why did you let her get to you?' Theo asked as they stowed the shopping in the boot of his car.

Could he really be that dense? Rosie closed her eyes and counted to ten. 'This is a small community and there's already been enough gossip about my family.'

She had no doubt there would be more after today. Miss Morris was a fast worker, and a word in her ear was more effective than taking out a full-page ad in one of the Sunday papers.

Theo shook his head. Rosie Farnham was a mass of contradictions — on the one hand, she was about as prickly as a hedgehog and overflowing with couldn't-care-less vibes and yet, on the other, she was obviously mortified by the prospect of a scandal.

'There are worse things than gossip.'

'And you're speaking from experience?'

'You learn not to care — to grow a thick skin.'

She shuddered visibly. 'There's not just me to consider,' she told him quietly. 'Evie's at an impressionable age.'

There was more to it, Theo was sure. But the journey back to the manor would take only a few minutes; not enough time to get to the bottom of the matter. No worries — there'd be many opportunities over the next few days to find out exactly what was going on in Rosie Farnham's head.

He powered the engine and turned the car back towards the estate. Rather disconcertingly, it already felt as if he was going home. He decided to ignore the feeling and pressed his foot on the accelerator. While there wasn't time for in-depth probing, he could use the journey to try to come to grips with the complicated family tree.

'How long ago did you lose your mother?' He glanced across in time to see Rosie bite her lip and wondered if perhaps he'd been tactless.

'She died giving birth to me,' Rosie answered after a moment. 'I never got the chance to get to know her, but I still miss her.'

'What about Harry's and Evie's mothers?'

'Harry's mother is still alive — but she, understandably, didn't have any time for me or Evie. Dad left them when Harry was a baby, and I think she's still bitter. And Evie's mother, Glory, disappeared shortly after Evie was born — we haven't seen or heard of her since.'

Theo drew the car up in front of the manor and glanced over to see Rosie's green eyes swimming with unshed tears. Something in his gut twisted. He was furious with himself. Only a complete idiot would have interrogated her with so little sensitivity.

He was overwhelmed by a yearning

to take her in his arms, to kiss away her tears, to promise her everything would be fine. He guessed she wouldn't thank him for it, though. In all honesty, he wouldn't thank himself, either — he'd never been fond of rescuing damsels in distress. He much preferred his women to be self-sufficient, especially emotionally. But something about Rosie made him behave in all sorts of strange ways.

* * *

Rosie threw the cash book down onto the desk. The task in hand was proving impossible.

She'd asked George to show Theo around the estate so she could go over the books without his very disturbing presence. Not that she'd put it in those terms — she did have the ability to be tactful when needed. She wanted everything to be in order. No, she *needed* everything to be in order. If she had any hope of persuading Theo that she'd be an asset as an employee, she had to impress on him how efficiently she'd run the estate. But however hard she tried, she just couldn't focus.

Shame burned her cheeks and she cringed inwardly as she tried to forget Miss Morris's less-than-subtle insinuations at the shop earlier.

Theo had insisted on accompanying her — wanted to see something of the village, he'd said. And, heaven help her, she'd had to let him pay for the groceries. Rosie hated to think what message that had given out. By now, Miss Morris had probably told the entire village that Rosie Farnham was a kept woman.

It might not have been so bad if he'd allowed her to drive in the estate's old Land Rover, as she normally would have done. But he'd insisted on taking her in his flashy black boy-toy car. It was sleek and expensive-looking — just like him. Nothing could have drawn more attention in such a small community.

Perhaps she wouldn't have found the

experience so shaming if she was entirely innocent, but the way she'd stared at Theo yesterday had been bordering on obscene. Her cheeks burned even more hotly. And he'd known — no way could he have missed it. Heaven help her, she'd been ogling him, she realised with distaste. Since Theo's appearance she'd behaved in all sorts of peculiar ways. Whoever knew that physical attraction could elicit such a strong reaction?

She only knew one thing with absolute certainty: it had to stop. She wanted a working relationship with Theo; a professional arrangement whereby she would run the estate for him and he'd allow her and Evie to stay on in return. On no account could she contemplate using feminine wiles to get her own way — she wasn't, and never had been, that sort of woman.

So what should she do?

Helplessly, she punched her brother's number into the phone again. Although it was mid-afternoon, she knew Harry would consider it an unearthly hour — Harry had turned nocturnal and tended to party until dawn. But she didn't care how annoyed he'd be if she woke him. She listened hopefully for the requisite number of rings, but there was no real surprise when the answering machine kicked in.

'Harry, this is Rosie. I need to speak to you urgently. Phone me back, please.'

Would he bother to call her back this time? Probably not. That lack of expectation weighed heavily on her as she turned back to the papers on the desk in front of her.

She frowned, unable to concentrate on the facts and figures as a sense of desolation engulfed her. The estate was the only life she'd known. How would she earn a living when Theo became fed up of this cat-and-mouse game and exerted his right to have her thrown out? She needed to feed and clothe Evie and keep a roof over their heads.

In addition, Evie had been distraught the only time Rosie had broached the subject of moving on. She'd pleaded and cried, explained that this was where her mother would look for her. A good few years had passed since then, but Rosie still recalled her sister's utter devastation — and that was why she'd battled so hard to keep things together.

Evie's ties to the place were even stronger now — the donkey sanctuary she'd set up meant the world to her. She hoped, eventually, to have it declared a charity and that volunteers would continue with the work when she went to university.

With a desperate sob, Rosie buried her face in her hands.

'Rosie?'

A very male voice broke into her despair. She snapped around to face him with such speed that she cricked her neck.

'How long have you been there?' she snapped.

She rubbed furiously at her eyes,

mortified that he'd caught her at such a vulnerable moment.

'Long enough.' He gave a half smile that might have been an apology and, despite her upset, Rosie's stomach fluttered.

'Haven't you better things to do than sneak up on people?'

'I did not sneak. I never sneak.'

'If you say so.' She sniffed and turned huffily back towards her work. Trust him to catch her crying! Noisily, she shuffled some papers on her desk. If she'd found it hard to concentrate with just the memory of Theo Bradley to keep her company, then the task would prove well-nigh impossible with the man himself in the same room. Infuriatingly, the warmth of a blush creep across her skin, turning her face as red as her nose must be.

'I have work to do,' she told him primly.

'Rosie.' He sighed softly. 'You don't need to do anything. I have a team who'll take care of it.'

Her shoulders slumped in utter defeat. There was no mistaking his message — she had no rights in this office any more. Bradley International Investments would appoint members of its own staff to oversee estate matters. Rosie was now redundant.

'You don't even know the extent of the overdraft.'

He seemed unconcerned and shrugged a broad shoulder. The action drew her attention to his body. Although he was casually dressed, the overall effect was so effortlessly elegant that Rosie had no doubt his outfit was designer. It was in stark contrast to her own bargain basement clothing — not that she was decrying bargain basement; without such outlets she'd have been roaming the estate in rags.

'I'm sure it's nothing that can't be dealt with.' He stepped closer and Rosie's heart thumped in her chest.

Really, this wasn't fair. She was so not interested in him as a man — so why did her body refuse to listen?

'Rosie?' He sat back on his heels and took her hands in his, much as he'd done yesterday. And, again, she was assailed by the need to lean forward and brush her lips against his. She pushed the thought to one side and concentrated, instead, on the fact this was the man who'd turned her life on its head.

'You have nothing to worry about,' he promised softly. 'I'll take care of everything.'

Her eyes clashed with his for just a moment — and then he slowly moved in for the kill.

His lips were firm, moving on hers with an assurance that left her reeling. She felt his kiss all the way down to her toes — and all the way back up again.

And then he drew back, but remained sitting on his heels in front of her, his hands on hers.

The kiss had been fleeting, but it left her dazed. She'd been unprepared for such intimacy with Theo, and never had she expected to enjoy it so much. The exotic taste of him, the tangy scent, had sent her senses into overdrive.

Rosie was disgusted with herself. She never allowed men to waltz into her home and kiss her. But the lessons she'd learned as she'd watched her father's countless liaisons — and how they cheapened the women who had adored him — had all been forgotten as Theo kissed her.

'Why did you do that?' she demanded. It was easier to blame him than to examine her own reactions.

He shrugged again. 'It seemed like the right thing to do. You were upset — I wanted to make you feel better. I didn't know what else to do.' He dropped her hands and got to his feet and she stared helplessly at him as he took a few steps away.

'It wasn't the right thing to do,' she told him quietly. 'We're in the middle of an almighty mess, and kissing doesn't have any place here.'

She could tell he didn't believe her as his gold eyes narrowed and his mouth twitched. He'd probably been able to work out how much she'd liked it — she hadn't pushed him away or anything. And, horror of horrors, she'd kissed him back — just for a moment, but her lips had definitely moved of their own accord.

She was the first to look away, turning her attention to the heap of untidy paperwork on the desk.

He cleared his throat. 'Why don't you give me a proper tour of the house? My plans were interrupted yesterday.'

He paused meaningfully, and guiltily she remembered exactly how she had interrupted those plans. If she thought she had a chance of getting away with throwing him out again, she might have been tempted into a repeat performance. Anything rather than having to deal with the complicated attraction she felt for him. Or seeing Theo's reaction when he finally saw her home in its inglorious entirety. She didn't want him to see how they lived — not when the reality was so depressing.

Rosie stared hopelessly at the papers scattered over her desk. 'But . . . '

'If you like, we could look over the accounts later.'

She shrugged, mentally admitting defeat. He'd officially relieved her of her other duties and there were no more excuses. Giving the paperwork one last, longing look, she got to her feet. 'I don't seem to have anything better to do.' And, she supposed, it would be best to move around the building, rather than sit in the confined office space, when the memory of his kiss was still so vivid.

To his credit, Theo said very little as they viewed the dilapidated rooms together. There was plenty he could have said — about the peeling wallpaper, the cracked plasterwork, the missing cornices and the dangerously dipping ceilings.

As they moved along the top floor landing, she heard an almighty clattering behind her and turned to find Theo lying sprawled across the threadbare carpet runner.

'Oh, my.' She rushed over and offered him a hand. 'I should have warned you to look out for the buckets.'

'What are they doing there?' He took her hand, but didn't burden her with his weight as he sprang effortlessly to his feet.

'We leak when it's wet,' she explained. 'The buckets are there to catch rainwater.'

It would be too easy to leave her hand nestled in his, but she pulled it away.

He ran his hand through his hair. 'I suppose I'd better add a new roof to the cost of renovations.'

Rosie knew he had to be mentally calculating the cost of repairs and refurbishment as they stepped over the debris. And she knew the total wouldn't bear thinking about. But still Theo didn't criticise, and she really liked him for that.

She would love the manor to be restored to its former splendid glory. It had been a beautiful house once, and it deserved to be taken care of. But she couldn't be happy with Theo's plans when her head was still buzzing with the news that he was planning to live at the manor. How could she hope that he'd let her and Evie stay, when he'd made it clear that he wanted the place to himself?

She still found it hard to accept the manor was no longer in the family. Of course, it had never actually belonged to Rosie in the first place. But while first her father and then Harry had held ownership, she'd believed she and Evie had an automatic right to a home here. Just showed how wrong a girl could be, she realised bitterly.

★　★　★

'Your brother seems to have effectively stripped every asset from the place,' Theo commented at last. He threw the estate cash books back onto the desk and picked up a folder of miscellaneous correspondence, flicking through it with lightning speed. His wish for a guided tour realised, he still hadn't said much, but Rosie had been able to tell from his grim expression that he wasn't in the least impressed by what he'd seen.

At her insistence, they then put in a horrific couple of hours going over the estate accounts. Sitting with only the old, rickety desk between them was doing her blood pressure few favours, but she didn't want it said that she'd hidden any of the unsavoury facts.

'Legally he's done nothing wrong.' Rosie grimaced, even to her own ears the excuse sounded pathetic.

'Perhaps — but all he's left is the shell of the property.'

'Why did you buy the estate without seeing it?' The question had been burning from the moment he'd turned up on the doorstep brandishing his ownership papers. According to the information Evie had uncovered, his reputation as an astute businessman was legendary. The Theo Bradley whose biography they had read on the net would not have thrown an inordinate amount of money at Harry for any rundown estate — especially when he hadn't seen the property in question.

'I didn't.' His expression was grim. 'You don't have a monopoly on feckless siblings.'

Rosie's brow furrowed. 'I don't follow.'

'Lysander,' he told her by way of explanation. 'My dear older brother. He met your brother through their mutual love of a good poker game. Harry had been losing heavily over a number of years — he sold out to cover his debts and Lysander was more than happy for Bradley Investments to foot the bill.'

7

Rosie slumped in her chair. It was almost as though she'd been slapped. Obviously, deep down, she'd held out some forlorn hope that Harry would ride to the rescue at some late hour — otherwise she wouldn't feel so crushed at this news.

Harry had a gambling habit and Rosie hadn't suspected. The startling truth was crushing. Even if she'd been able to convince Theo to sell the manor back to the family, Harry would not have had the money left to give him.

'You didn't know about Harry's gambling problem?'

Rosie shook her head. It seemed there was a lot she didn't know, and Theo was now wasting no time filling in the blanks.

'I thought as much when you suggested yesterday that he'd buy back the manor,' Theo surmised, his keen golden eyes scrutinising her horrified features. 'You should forget your brother, Rosie. His behaviour has been atrocious. Not only has he done nothing to help you raise Evie, but he's been actively working against you by plundering the estate assets to fund his party lifestyle.'

Rosie pushed back from the desk and began to pace the frayed carpet. 'Harry wasn't raised with us.' Despite agreeing with every word Theo said, she still needed to defend her brother. 'Dad didn't see him at all until he was an adult. He must have been jealous, felt he'd missed out on having a father around when he was growing up.'

Theo shook his head. 'He's a grown man — he should have got over any feelings of jealousy years ago. He should have helped you to run the estate when your father died. He should have taken responsibility for your sister.'

Rosie felt uncomfortable. Even if Harry was worse than useless, he was on her team — part of her family. While she was at liberty to complain about him, Harry's behaviour was none of Theo's business.

'I was happy to do it. I love my little sister. And I love this place. Besides, you should put your own brother in order before you start to criticise other people's.'

'I've dealt with Lysander. He no longer has access to any Bradley funds and he's been demoted to a position that even he'd find hard to mess up.'

Stunned, Rosie sat back down opposite this gorgeous man, looked across at his beautiful face and shivered. He was so cold as he spoke of his brother — his words so final that she felt the urge to shiver.

It did not bode well. If he was capable of treating a member of his own family like this, then throwing out two squatters from his newly acquired property would pose no problem.

He closed the file he had been reading with a slam.

'Don't look at me like that.'

'Like what?'

'Like I'm the big bad wolf in this story.'

She looked into his golden eyes and experienced a drowning sensation. He certainly posed as much danger as any fairytale villain, at least as far as she was concerned. She swallowed.

'Aren't you?'

Keep it professional, she reminded herself, *don't be so stupid*. She dragged her gaze away from Theo and settled instead on the framed poster of her father's band. Attitude! She sat up a little straighter in her chair.

Theo sighed. 'Rosie, none of this is of my doing. Our respective siblings got us into this mess.'

'But you could get us out of it.'

He ran a rough hand roughly though his hair. 'I'm flattered by your faith in my abilities, but this is a situation we're stuck with. I can't walk away, and it's obvious you can't, either.'

'I can't stay here — not without a

proper role.' Rosie took a deep breath. Time to convince him her plan could work. 'You could let me run the estate,' she pleaded. 'Let me and Evie stay at the manor and I'll turn this place around. You've seen the books, you know what I'm saying is true. If Harry's no longer allowed to help himself to the profits I could make this work.'

'Rosie — this place isn't fit for you and your sister to live in. It isn't fit for anyone.'

She got up and walked around the desk to face him.

'This is my home.'

No, it's not, a little voice reminded her. She told the voice to shut up. Theo had no right, no right at all to speak like this about the place she loved most.

'You know that Evie and I have lived here all our lives. We were both born here.'

'Times change. Things have to move on.'

'They don't have to,' she pleaded. 'You don't have to throw us out.'

'I've given you my word you have nothing to worry about, but I can't allow you and Evie to continue to live like this. Quite apart from my personal feelings on the matter, I'd be legally negligent in my duties as a landlord. This place isn't a suitable habitation for a dog, let alone two young women.'

Rosie was horrified. 'I can't believe you just said that.'

'It's true. You're deluding yourself if you think otherwise. The place is run down to a point where it poses a danger to life.'

'I've done my best to keep everything together. And you think you can waltz in and insult me and my home from your privileged, high and mighty position?'

'You need someone to make you face the truth.'

Such was Rosie's fury, Theo's face became a blur. She wanted to hurt him as he'd hurt her.

'I think I really hate you,' she told him quietly.

Something changed in the quality of

the way he looked at her. His eyes were fixed hungrily on her mouth. She realised too late what she'd done — after the effort of keeping things professional over the past few hours she'd lapsed, made it glaringly personal. She hadn't meant to cross boundaries with her carelessly uttered barb, but he obviously wasn't looking at things that way.

'I shouldn't have said that.' She backtracked. 'I didn't mean it. I'm sorry.'

'Too late.' He moved forward in his seat and she was transfixed by him, unable to move, unable to run as a sensible woman would have done. 'You're not forgiven.' He advanced, closer still, his mouth only inches from hers now. She could feel the warmth of his breath on her face, and that warmth filled her with longing. 'But, if you think you hate me, that must be the biggest delusion of all.'

More than anything she wanted to close the gap between them, but some level of sanity remained. She'd allowed him to kiss her earlier and she hadn't done a thing to stop him. But not this time! Theo was the enemy, who had plans to make her homeless and jobless — even if he insisted she had nothing to worry about. He was the man intent on leading her towards temptations that would make her no better than the women who'd partied with her father — the ones she'd pitied and despised as she'd been growing up. Her face burned.

'That's ridiculous. You're not my type!' The lie tripped off her tongue.

'Why not?'

'You're — too tall.' She uttered the first daft excuse to enter her head.

'That problem's not insurmountable.'

'You're talking in riddles — ' The sentence finished on a gasp as he gripped her around the waist and she tumbled down onto his lap. She pulled away at once and scrambled back to her feet.

'Not a good idea,' she told him primly, daring to look from beneath lowered eyelashes and noting he looked as shocked as she felt.

Theo couldn't explain what had happened. He'd never been so over-whelmed by a woman that all he could think about was kissing her again.

But Rosie had enjoyed their kiss every bit as much as he had, so why was she now being prickly? There was some-thing going on, he was sure — and it had to do with more than the estate. He ran an unsteady hand through his hair.

'Rosie!' The high-pitched cry made him whip round. A middle-aged woman swirled in, wearing an ankle-length dress of flowing purple, her long hair so blue-black it had to be dyed. Her eye make-up made her look rather like a panda.

'Marsha, I'm working,' Rosie mut-tered. 'It will have to wait.'

'It can't, darling. Really it can't. I was speaking to Alicia on the telephone this afternoon . . .'

Rosie turned towards Theo. 'Alicia Powell,' she explained. 'She was married to Adam, The Noise's lead guitarist.' Rosie used her warning tone, he noticed, and he suspected she was trying to stop the older woman from rambling on. 'This is Marsha,' she told Theo. 'George's mother. And this,' she told Marsha, 'is Theo Bradley.'

'Delighted.' Marsha's wide red-lipsticked smile scared him witless. 'I'm Marsha Barton.' He took the hand she offered with caution — quite rightly as it turned out, as she used the contact to pull him closer and smack a noisy kiss full on his lips. His nose twitched at the overpowering effect of her perfume.

Startled, he sprang back out of harm's way. At least his reaction confirmed he wasn't turning into some out-of-control predator — it was only Rosie who tempted him to let down his defences.

'So, what about Alicia?' Rosie sounded irritated and he hoped mischievously that it was because she didn't like another woman kissing him — even if it was clearly a theatrical gesture that Marsha probably made to everyone she met.

'Fabulous news, darling — she wants to come home to us. I told her we must have a party . . . '

'That is good news,' Rosie agreed.

'I thought you might be able to let her stay at Farnham House — I know it's been empty since . . . well . . . since your father died. But it's a good distance away from that awful Adam man — honestly, the way he treated that woman I can't begin to understand,' she said shaking her head.

'It won't be possible for Alicia to stay at Farnham House,' Theo interrupted and was rewarded by two pairs of female eyes pinning him quizzically in place. 'I have plans for that place already. If Alicia Powell's coming back to the estate, she'll have to make do with one of the empty cottages.'

'I don't know who you are, Theo Bradley, but I was speaking to Rosie.

This has nothing to do with you.'

Theo let his breath out in a loud hiss. Not accustomed to having his authority questioned, he began to wonder if there was something in the water on the Farnham estate that made its females overly feisty.

There was an unmistakable warning in Rosie's green eyes and the shake of her head was barely perceptible as she silently warned him to say nothing. Of course, she hadn't told her sister yet — she wouldn't want him to announce he was the new owner.

'Marsha, there's no need to be rude.' Rosie's voice was strained. 'Why don't you get Alicia to give me a ring to discuss where she can stay?'

Marsha flounced out in a huff and Rosie turned to face him. 'Thank you for not saying anything.'

He nodded briefly. 'She seems a bit, er, high maintenance.'

Rosie's short laugh held no humour. 'That's one way of putting it.'

'You prefer another way?'

'Marsha and her husband are a bit of a nightmare. The band got together when they were very young and the manager treated them all like children. And then they moved onto the estate and expected Dad to take care of them. They've never really grown up — and everything's a drama in their world.'

'And nobody's putting a stop to it?'

'What can we do? It's the way they are. But it's George I feel sorry for — he's thinking of giving up a place at music college to stay and take care of them. He worries about them.'

As someone who had of necessity taken care of himself from a young age, Theo was shocked. He knew that something should be done, particularly with George having to bear the burden of his parents' irrational dependency. But, like Rosie, he had no idea what.

'What are you planning for Farnham House?' she asked, bringing him away from his thoughts.

'I had a good look at it earlier, when George showed me around. Structurally it's sound — definitely in better condition than the manor.'

He watched as she bit her lower lip. 'Dad kept it in fairly good order because that was where his girlfriends stayed. He didn't want them in the manor — I don't know if that was to protect me and Evie, or if he was ashamed of the state the building was in and it was easier to keep the house in order because it's so much smaller.'

Theo suspected the latter. He was sure, from what he'd heard, Mick Farnham would only have had his own best interests at heart, but he said nothing on the matter — no point when the man was long dead.

'I've got a team moving in tomorrow,' he explained. 'They're going to give the place a bit of a facelift. It's mostly cosmetic, but they're going to make it habitable for you and Evie.'

'No. I couldn't possibly . . . '

'You can't stay here, Rosie.'

'But Farnham House — ' Her nose wrinkled in distaste. Despite having lived on the estate all her life, she'd never been inside that house. As far as she was concerned, it was a place of sin and she had no desire to see it, let alone live in it.

'The manor's going to have to undergo a complete renovation and, while it's all going on, things aren't going to be too pretty here. You could, of course, move into one of the cottages, but if you're going to manage the place for me I think you should be away from the tenants.'

'What?' She was sure she couldn't have heard him correctly.

'I think you should live away from the tenants.'

'No . . . ' She almost screamed with frustration. 'What did you say before that?'

He hesitated and she could have thrown something at his handsome head. ''If you're going to manage the place' . . . '

She stared at him for a moment before she took a running jump across the faded tiling of the office floor and threw herself at him, wound her arms around his neck and hugged him tight. As her face burrowed into his warm neck, the smell of his aftershave drawing her closer, she felt him still in shock. Not surprising — she was a little shocked herself. And then his arms came around her and he hugged her back.

'You mean it?'

'I'd never joke about something like that.'

Rosie was completely embarrassed to feel the threat of tears stinging at her eyes. But, really, Theo could have no idea of how much this meant to her. With this job offer, she and Evie now had the right to stay on the estate — they would have a proper place here, without fear of eviction. Even if it did mean they'd have to move away from the manor . . . and to the house her father had kept for his mistresses.

Realising she was still hugging him tightly, she became aware of a blush spreading over her entire body. She shouldn't have done this, thrown herself at him. What must he think of her? She was suddenly supremely aware of how warm he felt, how strong his arms were around her — and how deliciously wonderful it felt to be held by him. Finding it hard to breathe, she let him go and slid down until her feet hit the floor.

'Thank you,' she told him, trying bravely not to cry through a mixture of gratitude, relief and complete mortification.

'It's not a favour, Rosie. I really think you're the best person for the job. I'll be going back to my real life soon and I need someone I can trust here. You're the obvious choice — you're hard-working, you're dedicated and you love the place.'

She wiped fiercely at her eyes with the back of her hands as she lost her battle to hold back the tears.

'I suppose I'd better speak to Evie.'

She still didn't know how her sister

was going to take the news, but at least now Rosie had a concrete and positive solution to offer when she revealed they would have to leave the manor.

Theo stepped closer and lifted his hand uncertainly, as though he was going to wipe the tears from her cheek, before dropping it down by his side again.

'Don't cry, Rosie, please. This was supposed to make you happy — to reassure you that you had a future here for as long as I own the estate.'

She sniffed loudly. 'I'm sorry. I just can't believe you're letting us stay.'

He shrugged helplessly and she made a monumental effort to regain her composure. Rosie never lost her cool like this — no one had ever seen her cry. No matter how difficult the circumstances had been, she hadn't allowed herself to shed tears in front of anyone. And yet, in their short acquaintance, Theo Bradley had witnessed her loss of composure on more than one occasion.

'I'll speak to Evie after tea,' she promised.

8

Considering how adamant she'd always been that she wanted to stay at the manor, Evie was remarkably calm when Rosie broke the news as they cleared the dinner things.

'The house is still on the estate,' she reasoned in response to Rosie wondering aloud about the change in Evie's priorities.

'So your mum will be able to find you if she comes back.'

It was years since Evie had spoken about her mother, Glory, but Rosie knew that she must still hope.

'I'm not waiting for her to turn up any more,' Evie replied matter-of-factly as she carried on with the washing-up. 'I was thinking more of the sanctuary. I need to be on the estate — or close by, at least, for the donkeys.'

'I, er, haven't quite squared with

Theo that we can keep the sanctuary.' With the admission, Rosie avoided her sister's gaze.

There was a loud splash as Evie dropped a cup into the soapy water. 'What?'

'I was too busy trying to secure our future. I haven't actually spoken to him about the future of the sanctuary yet.' Although, judging by his reaction when he'd found out about the donkeys, she didn't hold out much hope. Not that she was going to push him on the issue — he'd already conceded more than she could ever have hoped by offering her a job and a home.

Ridiculous though it sounded after her initial adverse reaction, she was beginning to like Theo Bradley. And his acquiring the estate could only be a good thing — whether the donkeys were allowed to stay or not. The place would be renovated and would thrive as profits from the fruit and tree crops were reinvested.

'I'll speak to him,' Evie announced,

drying her hands on a tea towel. 'Where is he?'

'You can't disturb him, he's working. You can talk to him tomorrow.' But Rosie found she was talking to Evie's retreating back as her sister headed off in the direction of the office.

With a sigh she walked to the sink and picked up the washing-up brush. She couldn't be cross because, in Evie's position, she would have done exactly the same thing. But she did wonder if Theo had had any idea what he'd been letting himself in for when he decided to take on the Farnham women.

* * *

Rosie had guessed it wouldn't take long for news of Theo's stay at the Manor to spread. Her desire for discretion didn't stand a chance against Miss Morris — and a younger sister who had a foghorn where her mouth should be.

She didn't, however, expect to see

Julia in her office, just after lunch the next day.

'I thought Sunday afternoon was your family time.'

'I've only popped over for five minutes.' Julia tucked a strand of her short blonde hair behind her ear as she flopped into the chair across the desk from Rosie. 'Bob and Louise are getting to grips with tidying up the lunch things, so I thought I'd try to find out about this man you've moved into the manor.'

Rosie sighed. Having friends was one thing, but she was tired of not being able to so much as sneeze without it being discussed in minute detail by everyone within a five-mile radius.

'I haven't moved a man in.'

'Really?' Julia looked so disappointed, Rosie would have laughed — if she wasn't so annoyed.

'Theo hasn't moved in. He's only staying for a while to get to grips with the workings of the estate.'

Julie's eyes narrowed. 'That's not

usually how these things work, I'm sure.'

Rosie shrugged helplessly. 'What could I do? He insisted and he owns the place.'

'I heard he's hot.'

'So Evie tells me.'

Julia laughed. 'Come on, Rosie. I know you've been living like a nun, but even you must know whether a man's good-looking.'

'Okay.' Rosie felt her cheeks glow. 'He's good-looking.'

'Evie said he was *very* good-looking.' A wicked grin.

'Okay, he's *very* good-looking. And hot, in fact. Happy now?'

'So, we've established he's here, he's attractive. Is he also single?'

Rosie could see exactly where this conversation was going and she didn't like it. 'Yes,' she muttered.

'Then what are you waiting for?'

She stared her friend straight in the eye. Julia knew better than anyone why Rosie avoided romantic entanglements.

'I've already had this conversation with Evie. I'm not looking for a man.'

'It doesn't have to be anything serious. Just a fling.'

Rosie tried not to shudder. Her father had never had anything serious with any of his women — not even the ones he'd married.

'I don't have flings,' she declared, in much the same way she'd told Evie that she didn't snog.

But no-strings flings and snogging had never seemed as attractive as they did with Theo Bradley under the same roof.

*　*　*

Of all the places Theo might have expected to be on a Sunday afternoon, taking care of a bunch of donkeys would have seemed the least likely. But that was before he'd met Rosie Farnham and her equally persuasive sister.

The younger Farnham had arrived at

129

the estate office like a whirlwind last night and suggested his help would be very much appreciated. 'None of the usual volunteers can make it tomorrow,' she said.

'What about George?' he'd asked desperately.

'Too busy,' she replied cheerfully. 'He puts in all the hours he can on the estate and doesn't really have time to help me.'

'But he does sometimes?'

She nodded. 'But he's way too busy this weekend.'

Theo had suspected an ulterior motive — and he guessed it would have something to do with convincing him to keep the sanctuary open.

As they arrived in the meadow, five pairs of curious eyes watched them approach.

'They recognise you?' He was amazed as he watched the animals nuzzle closer.

'Of course.' She laughed, patting each soft head in turn. 'They're very intelligent animals.'

'What made you set up the sanctuary?'

'Two of the tenants on the estate left Jessie behind when they moved on. We kept waiting for them to come back for her, but they never did. And she became a bit of a pet. One day, we heard of another donkey — Flora — looking for a home. We thought she'd be company for Jessie. The others were just sort of added along the way. Izzy and Chloe are sisters and arrived together. And, last of all, Mr Kennedy.'

'There must be a great deal of work involved,' Theo said. 'Cost, too.' He frowned. Rosie was struggling to keep food on the table; on what planet was it a good idea to introduce the upkeep of expensive animals into the mix?

She nodded. 'It is hard work, but worth it. Me and my friend Louise run the place — and we've recruited some volunteers who help out. We try to keep expenses to a minimum. Luckily, they don't eat much. And Louise's dad is a vet, so he's agreed to look after the donkeys free of charge.'

'I see.' Theo could well imagine how Louise's father might have been coerced into helping. If her friend was as forceful as Evie, he reckoned the poor man wouldn't have stood a chance. He accepted the brush she handed him and stood uncertainly, not quite knowing what to do.

'That's for grooming,' she explained patiently, as she tied one of the animals — a small brown creature — to a fence post. 'And this is Flora. She'll keep nice and still for you now, while you brush her.'

He glanced uncertainly from brush to Flora and back again. This was not on his list of things to do today.

'She won't bite.' Evie laughed as she took hold of his arm and pulled him over. 'Some of them do, but not this one. We'll start you off nice and gently.'

Start him off . . . ? As far as Theo was concerned this would be the start and the end of it. He was too busy to make this a regular occurrence.

'Does Rosie ever help you with the sanctuary?'

The question had been as casual as he was able to make it, but at the mention of her sister, Evie's head snapped around.

'Sometimes,' she admitted, her perceptive blue eyes watching him closely. 'She says she has better things to do with her time, but at heart she's a real softie. I know she loves the donkeys as much as I do.'

Theo couldn't help the smile that tugged at his lips. Rosie, he guessed, would not appreciate being described as a softie.

He was aware of Evie looking at him thoughtfully. 'I don't know if I should say this, I mean she'll like totally kill me if she finds out . . . '

'Finds out what?'

'It's just . . . I think she likes you.'

Theo felt the corners of his mouth tug again.

'That's good. I like her.'

'No,' Evie was insistent. 'I mean she

really likes you.'

If Evie was telling the truth, he'd have to put Rosie straight. It was only fair. He couldn't allow her to expect, to hope . . .

'But the thing is, she's scared.' Evie paused and then spoke in a rush again. 'I'm saying too much. You mustn't tell her any of this.'

He felt he couldn't breathe. 'I wouldn't dream of it.' Absently, he began to brush the unsuspecting Flora. The last thing he wanted was to hurt Rosie. But he didn't want a permanent romantic relationship — he'd decided that a long time ago.

'The thing is, Rosie is complicated.'

That was nothing he hadn't worked out for himself.

'She's brave and she's beautiful, but she's a bit rubbish at commitment. Because of the way Dad behaved, she never wants to get married. Or even be tied into a serious relationship.'

Theo only just resisted the urge to sigh with relief. Rosie Farnham was on his wavelength. The weight in his chest eased and he found he was able to breathe again.

'So you mustn't let yourself get too attached,' Evie continued. 'I've encouraged her to go out with you — to have some fun, because she never has any fun and I'm worried about her. But I can see you like her, too. And she won't mean to hurt you, but she just can't bring herself to commit to a man.'

Only then did he realise Evie wasn't concerned about her sister's heart; it was *his* emotions she feared for. He was unbelievably touched; no one had ever worried about him before.

'Thank you, Evie,' he told her sincerely. 'I'll make sure I look out for myself and won't take your sister too seriously.'

She nodded. 'Good. So you'll ask her out?'

'Maybe I will.' He smiled. The thought of bringing some uncomplicated fun into Rosie's life appealed very much indeed.

Evie smiled back. 'This is Mr Kennedy.' She introduced a little grey donkey and began to brush him. 'He hasn't been with us very long.'

'Isn't Mr Kennedy a strange name for a donkey?'

He watched as she wrinkled her nose. 'I suppose it is. I hadn't thought about it.'

As he watched her work, brushing the donkeys, clearing out their small barn, Theo couldn't help being impressed. Evie was obviously a young woman with drive and ambition, and she wasn't afraid of hard work.

'So now you've seen the sanctuary, what do you think?' she asked as they walked back. 'Can the donkeys stay?'

It made no economic sense to keep the donkeys. In fact it made as little sense as it did to keep the manor. With a sigh, he made his decision.

'The donkeys can stay.'

He was practically deafened by a squeal he was sure must be well over the safe decibel level.

* * *

Rosie had never imagined Theo could look so dishevelled as he did when he arrived back in the office in the early evening. 'Evie kept you busy, I see,' she commented as she took in the mud and the general air of disarray.

He glanced at his clothes and grimaced. 'You've no idea. That girl is a whirlwind. We've scrubbed the barn, brushed several donkeys, cleared some of the overgrowth in the adjoining land . . . '

Rosie smiled. It seemed her little sister knew exactly how to negotiate with the uber-successful Theo Bradley. 'Don't tell me she talked you into giving her that extra piece of land so she can expand the sanctuary?'

'She has. Although I'm not quite sure how.'

Rosie laughed. 'It's teen talk,' she told him. 'She's an expert. Has you tied up in circles and agreeing to things before you know it.'

Theo grinned and consulted his watch. 'Are you hungry? Evie said she was eating at her friend Louise's tonight. Why don't we have dinner at Chudley House to celebrate your new job?'

Rosie would much rather spend the time working on the plans she needed to make for the estate. But they'd begun their working relationship with so much antagonism, she didn't need to add to it by picking petty arguments. She briefly nodded her agreement to the dinner plan. 'But I'm paying half,' she insisted before remembering she had no money. 'Well — I'll pay you back when I get my first pay cheque.'

He shook his head. 'I own the place — we won't have to pay.'

Rosie sighed noisily, but didn't argue further. Whatever she said would only make her sound childish. 'Well, if you say so.'

'We should get ready. I'll meet you in the hall in fifteen minutes. Is that enough time?'

Get ready? Horror struck at Rosie's

heart. She'd need to get changed — Chudley House was seriously posh. What could she wear? As sole guardian to Evie and full-time estate manager, she rarely got the chance to go out on social occasions and her wardrobe reflected this. Normally it didn't bother her, but there was no way her usual garb of jeans and T-shirt would do this evening. She needed something dressy. Heck.

Quickly she pinned her hair up, took the fastest shower in history and then dug out the only possibility in her wardrobe — a little black dress, gifted by Julia and her family for her last birthday along with a pair of black killer heels. She hated the outfit but had worn it to the surprise dinner they'd arranged, not wanting to hurt her friends. She'd spent the entire evening loathing the way the dress clung, and its low neckline. She'd been sure everyone was staring at her and had vowed she'd never willingly wear the garment again. Needs must, though — and her outing with Theo left her with little choice.

9

Rosie appeared only a minute after the designated meeting time. Theo would have been impressed — no other woman of his acquaintance had even come close to getting ready in such a short space of time — but the vision descending the stairs towards him dazzled every coherent thought from his mind.

She'd pinned her hair up, but nonetheless, coppery curls had escaped to frame her face. The dress was something else — propelling her from an already stunning beauty into a league all her own.

He remained rooted to the spot. He wished he hadn't made the rash promise to take her out to dinner as another, much more fun way to celebrate her new job occurred to him. He longed to take her in his arms, to once again feel the passionate response from her as he kissed her.

He exhaled sharply. What had happened to him since he'd stepped over the threshold of Farnham Manor only the day before yesterday? He had never been less in control, and he didn't like it. He preferred his relationship with women to be strictly unemotional. He had been in control of his feelings every second he had spent with Gina and her predecessors. As far as he was concerned, it was a necessary form of self-preservation. Falling in love was dangerous, it wasn't nice — he'd grown up with the example of what happened when love turned sour, and that wasn't what he wanted for himself.

So it was just as well that he wasn't falling in love with Rosie Farnham. Physical attraction — that's what it amounted to. It had nothing at all to do with the dangerous emotion that scared him so much.

★   ★   ★

All the way to Chudley House, Rosie sat in the passenger seat of Theo's car feigning what she hoped was a cool exterior, while her insides churned with awareness. She was horribly self-conscious in the dress she felt was too tight, too short and too low, and couldn't believe that Julia had chosen it for her.

Sometimes she felt her friend barely knew her at all. And it wasn't only this unsuitable choice of present. She was still reeling from Julia's suggestion earlier. Fancy suggesting Rosie enjoy a *fling* with Theo, for Heaven's sake.

She shifted in her seat as she became aware of Theo glancing over. She felt completely exposed, and hated the way her heart rate increased every time he cast a look her way.

Despite wishing it otherwise, she couldn't deny the deep physical attraction between them. If she forced herself to be honest, she'd thoroughly enjoyed his kiss. Her face burned even now at the memory.

She tried to think of other things, to take her mind off the masculine thighs, only inches from hers, from the strong, brown hands braced on the steering wheel . . . He looked breathtakingly spectacular this evening — dressed in a grey suit and a white shirt, he oozed masculine charisma from the top of his black-as-night hair to the toes of his undoubtedly expensive leather shoes. *Forget he's a man*, she reminded herself in a desperate attempt at self-defence.

Huh — no chance. They didn't come any more manly than Theo Bradley.

From her reaction to him, she had to face the uncomfortable truth that there was very little difference between her and those women who used to hang around the manor. The iron self-control she'd expected she would exercise, should she ever be faced with something like this, had been nothing more than a figment of her imagination.

She took a deep breath and made a conscious effort to block out Theo Bradley and the effect he had on her.

Instead, she thought about Chudley House Hotel and how she was looking forward to seeing it. Even Rosie had heard of the exclusive establishment. She'd even read about it on the odd occasion she'd picked up one of Evie's magazines and found some celebrity or other had graced the place with their presence. Having never expected to go there herself, however, she'd taken little notice.

'The original house was demolished years ago,' Theo explained as the car purred up the extensive driveway and a breathtaking modern building came into view. 'We bought the land because the setting is stunning.'

That was no exaggeration. Set in acres of lush countryside, there could be few places to match it in terms of its stunning views over the soft rolling hills.

Theo proved to be an expert guide, pointing out all the exclusive touches that made this place special.

'It's all lovely,' she told him. And it

was. The design and furnishings were breathtaking. The staff had been unobtrusive but solicitous.

And the food was to die for. 'I can understand why everyone raves about it,' she told Theo with a soft sigh as their main course was cleared away.

He scrutinised her expression shrewdly. 'But . . . ?'

'But Chudley House is entirely new. It doesn't really give me any idea of what you'll do with the manor. I know it's really none of my business, but you promised a renovation, not a demolition. How do I know your renovation will be sympathetic?' She knew that, as only an employee, she had no right to ask, but she needed to know what he had planned.

He reached out and uncurled her fingers from where they were tightly wound around the stem of her wine glass. Absently stroking the palm of her hand with his thumb, he looked intently into her eyes. 'Do you trust me, Rosie?'

Rosie gulped. She hadn't expected

him to ask her that. She thought for only a moment before she realised in amazement that she did trust him — very odd as they'd only just met, and Rosie's default setting was to be suspicious of everyone.

Mouth dry, she was unable to speak, so she nodded and saw his full lips curve into a brief smile before he brought her hand up to offer a whisper of a kiss against her fingers. She nearly passed out with the electric reaction. She closed her eyes against the confusing mixture of emotions assaulting her.

'There are experts on my team who have already effected very sympathetic renovations of some of my older properties,' he assured her quietly. 'I only employ the best — the manor will be in good hands.'

She opened her eyes. A hopeful smile dawned as it hit her that Theo could be relied on to look after the home that had meant so much to her father. A burden was lifted from her shoulders.

For the first time in her life, she truly felt that she didn't need to worry about the manor. And she trusted that Theo wouldn't let her down.

'How did you end up with responsibility for Evie?' he asked as they ate pudding.

She swallowed a mouthful of chocolate mousse and looked at him in surprise. It hadn't occurred to her she would have to explain. 'There was nobody else.'

'There's always someone else.'

'Not in this case,' she insisted. 'Besides, I wanted to do it. I was there when she was born. In fact, I delivered her.'

'How did you know what to do?'

Theo looked as appalled as he sounded and Rosie resisted the urge to laugh at his reaction — it had been no laughing matter. In fact it had been a pretty scary situation for them all.

'I didn't, but Glory hadn't realised she was in labour until the last minute and it was too late to get help. I had no choice.'

It had been the worst night of her life — two lives depending on her, and she hadn't been remotely prepared. And the shadow of what had happened to Rosie's own mother had loomed large. She'd been so scared that Glory and her baby — Evie — might die.

The medical staff, who had arrived shortly after the birth, told her she'd done a great job, but she still wasn't sure. If she hadn't panicked, if she'd been more supportive, if she'd known what she was supposed to do . . . If things had been different, perhaps Glory might have stayed and all their lives would have been better.

Even in retrospect and from the perspective of a grown woman, she was unable to look back on that night without feeling that she was, somehow, to blame for Glory's decision to leave the family.

'Where was your father that night?'

'Dad had gone out, we didn't know where. He didn't come back for days.'

'That must have been hard on you.'

'It was. But, from the moment I first held the baby in my arms I fell in love with her. Everyone used to laugh because I treated her like some sort of doll, took her everywhere, stayed off school to mind her. But with Glory gone and Dad not interested in her, she was more like my child than my sister.'

'You were practically still a child yourself.'

'I was sixteen, but it's surprising how quickly you have to grow up when you have responsibilities.'

He was quiet for a moment. She thought he might confide something, but the moment passed and he reached out instead.

'Come, dance with me.' He took her hand and rose to his feet, taking her with him towards the dimly-lit dance floor.

He drew her into his arms and cradled her against his body. She reached up to link her fingers at the back of his neck, playing absently with the hair that curled into his nape. It was amazing how right it seemed, and she knew a moment of satisfaction as he shivered against her. She closed her eyes and leaned closer, feeling an unfamiliar surge of utter contentment begin to carry her away . . .

'Well, well, look who it is.' A smarmy male voice broke into their private world, shattering the moment. 'How very cosy. Aren't you going to introduce me to your little friend?'

The effect couldn't have been more drastic if the newcomer had thrown a bucket of iced water over them. Theo immediately dropped his hold and sprang round to confront the intruder.

'What the hell are you doing here? I thought I told you to stay away from me for the foreseeable future.'

'What a way to greet your big brother.'

So this was Theo's brother. Rosie would never have picked him out, because the two could not have been more different. Whereas Theo was tall, muscular and dark, his brother was significantly shorter, slighter and paler. Not surprising, really — quite apart from Theo being a definite one-off, Rosie knew from her experience that siblings sometimes looked nothing alike. She herself was a short redhead, Evie was tall and blonde and Harry mousey, balding and overweight — three half-siblings who looked as though they came from totally different gene pools.

'Tell me what you want, then get lost.' Theo could not hide his annoyance.

Rosie watched with morbid fascination. It was obvious there was no love lost between the two, and seeing their relationship first hand was nothing short of chilling.

'I saw Gina yesterday. She told me about your engagement. She's understandably ecstatic she's managed to snare you at last. I wonder what she would say if she knew you were being so . . . *friendly* with another woman,' Lysander mused maliciously.

Nothing he could have said could

have had more of an effect on Rosie. Theo had kissed her, taken her out to dinner and danced with her — all when he already had an unsuspecting fiancée lined up. And it was all her own fault — she knew what men could be like, and she'd still dropped her guard and allowed herself to be carried along on the crest of his lies.

He was engaged to another woman.

Revulsion surged upwards from her toes and spread up through her body. When he'd been kissing Rosie, making her believe he found her attractive, dancing with her, he hadn't been free to do any of those things.

Feeling sick, she tottered on her too-high heels towards the exit. She hated him. Her initial instincts had been right. Thirty-six short hours ago, she'd been blissfully unaware of his existence. Now, he had torn her peace of mind to shreds and had cast her in the role of the other woman — a role she would rather have died than entered into.

She crashed through the doors and staggered outside, where she was grateful to find a breeze brushing against her overheated cheeks. But the area was bustling with arriving and departing guests, and Rosie needed solitude, so she walked around the side of the building and down into the fragrant and colourful gardens.

She knew that, in reality, very little had actually happened between herself and Theo, other than a brief kiss and some scorching glances. But Theo most certainly had no business kissing another woman the way he had kissed Rosie, or holding her so closely as they danced — not when he had a fiancée.

Despite the cool evening air, her face burned even more hotly. She was furious. Why had she relaxed her guard? She barely knew him and yet she'd allowed him to get beneath her armour, closer to the core of her than anyone else had ever done.

She sat on a secluded bench, hidden from the majority of the visitors to the garden by bushes. She was too upset to take in her surroundings, and she attempted several deep, laboured breaths in an attempt to ease the pain in her chest.

It hurt. It physically hurt. And she couldn't believe someone she'd known for such a short time could cause such havoc with her wellbeing.

She was still gasping for breath when he arrived in a fury — six foot four of brooding manhood bearing down on her, his eyes dark with anger.

'I need to be on my own,' she managed. 'Go away.'

But he didn't. He stood his ground, taking his eyes from her only to acknowledge two elderly ladies who were looking on the scene with interest as they passed nearby.

'Good evening.' Theo rewarded them with his killer smile.

'Hello,' they spoke in unison and giggled happily at the attention as they continued on their way.

Rosie turned away in disgust from the spectacle of the ladies nearly swooning in response, conveniently forgetting the effect Theo's charm elicited when it was turned on her.

The smile faded as though a switch had been flicked as he turned his attention back on Rosie.

'Don't ever run out on me again,' he growled.

The warning in his voice was unmistakable, but Rosie refused to be intimidated. She got to her feet and stood her ground, hands on hips, her lethal heels giving her valuable extra inches.

'Don't ever cheat on your fiancée with me again,' she countered, barely able to form the words.

He raked an impatient hand through his black hair. 'I haven't cheated on anyone with you.'

'You're engaged to someone else but you kissed me. You brought me to dinner. You danced with me. If my fiancé did any of those things with another woman I'd be pretty upset. How could you not tell me you were engaged to someone else?'

'For a very simple reason: I'm not.'

She snorted. 'Your brother just said . . . '

'My brother is an idiot and a liar. I demoted him because of his incompetence in the business and now he's trying to get back at me by causing trouble.'

'So there's nobody called Gina in your life?'

'There was a Gina, once. But that was all over long before I met you. She knows it. I know it. And now, so do you.'

She wanted to believe him. She wanted to believe him so badly. But years of conditioning, years of watching her father treating women badly, were hard to forget.

'How do I know you're telling me the truth?'

'I never lie.' He looked her squarely in the eye — liquid gold clashing with sea green. And, despite barely knowing him, she believed him. The realisation overwhelmed her. She inclined her head in the briefest of nods and he relaxed visibly.

'Lysander's now been sacked and escorted from the premises. If we never lay eyes on him again it won't be any great loss.' His gaze remained unflinching. 'Do you believe me?'

She was shocked to realise she did. 'Yes.' Her voice was barely a whisper.

'Good.' He stared at her for a long moment before giving a short nod and reaching out to tuck his hand beneath her elbow. 'Come on, let's go home.'

10

Evie was waiting outside for them when they arrived back. 'I'm really worried about Flora,' she said, frowning.

'Why? What's the matter with her?' Rosie said as she struggled out of the passenger seat of Theo's car and tottered towards the house.

'I'm not sure. She's lying on her side, groaning. I think it might be colic.'

Rosie bit her lip. This wasn't good. Evie had been around the donkeys long enough for her instinct about the animals to be very good.

'Okay, I'll change my shoes then head up to the sanctuary, see if I can't get her moving. You give Bob a ring and tell him I'll meet him there.'

Things looked bad when Rosie arrived at the field. Flora was rolling on the ground in obvious agony. In Rosie's opinion, Evie's diagnosis had been correct. She wished Bob would hurry up — Flora needed an injection to relax her muscles, and fast.

In the meantime, she had to get the animal moving.

'Come on sweetheart,' Rosie coaxed, still in her little black dress, but now also wearing a fetching pair of wellies. 'Let's get you to your feet.' The other donkeys stood by, watching in silence as Rosie tried to persuade Flora to her feet.

She needed to walk Flora around the field, but the animal refused to co-operate. She continued to writhe on the grass. 'Please,' Rosie whispered in one brown, furry ear. 'You need to stop doing that.'

She was still trying to persuade the donkey to her feet when Theo and Evie arrived. 'Bob wasn't in,' her sister revealed through her tears. 'I've left a message with Julia. She says she'll send him over as soon as he gets back.'

Rosie nodded. 'I need to get Flora to her feet,' she told Theo. 'If I can get her moving we might be able to dislodge the gas that's bothering her. But if I can't . . . '

'What will happen?' For someone who hadn't been mad keen on the donkeys, Theo was looking very concerned.

Rosie bit her lip. She didn't want to say it out loud.

'She might end up with a twisted gut,' Evie replied. 'And then there'll be nothing any of us can do.'

Theo got to his knees and began to speak softly to the distressed donkey. It took a while, but he eventually managed to persuade Flora to her feet.

'I don't believe it,' Rosie muttered. But, despite her words, she couldn't help smiling. 'Are there *any* females on the planet you can't charm?'

'There is one who's intent on resisting me.' He flashed a brief smile back. 'But Flora and I are old friends.'

Flora wasn't out of the woods — not even nearly. But at least she was on her feet and one step closer to being saved.

Muttering words of reassurance, Rosie led her around.

'Look at that,' Theo commented in wonder. Rosie turned to find the other donkeys followed behind as she walked with Flora. 'It's almost as though they know how ill she is and want to offer some support.'

'They understand,' Rosie explained. 'We've been through this before — and they always behave in the same way.'

Flora was still in obvious pain — her movements awkward and laboured. But, after a while, she seemed a little less distressed. 'There's still a way to go, but I think . . . ' Rosie took a deep breath, hardly daring to articulate her hope. 'I think she's going to be okay.'

'Thank goodness.' Evie sighed in obvious relief.

'It's going to be a very long night. Why don't you and Theo go back to the manor?' she suggested. 'I'm going to stay and keep her walking.'

'It's okay,' Evie insisted. 'I'd rather stay.'

161

'Evie, it's late — and it's a school night.'

'Look,' Theo broke in. 'Why don't the two of you go back and I'll walk with Flora — at least until Bob gets here? If there's any change for the worse I'll ring you straight away.'

'But . . . ' Rosie and Evie complained in unison.

'There's no point us all being out here all night,' he argued reasonably. 'And Rosie, you're not really dressed for a night out in the fields.'

She didn't want to go. Theo was a city boy — with a business brain. Leaving him in charge of a sick donkey didn't seem very fair or sensible.

His business brain picked up on her concern. 'I'm capable of walking Flora,' he told her quietly. 'Trust me.'

She found that she did. Besides, Evie seemed more than happy to leave her beloved Flora in his care, so Rosie went back to the manor with her. But once she'd seen Evie safely indoors, she hurriedly changed into jeans and a

162

jumper, made up a flask of hot coffee and went back out to join him.

Bob was just leaving as Rosie arrived back at the sanctuary. 'How is Flora?' she asked the vet anxiously.

'Over the worst,' he replied. 'You've done a great job.' He looked over his shoulder at Theo. 'All of you.'

Rosie glanced over to where Theo still led the procession of donkeys. Her gaze clashed with flashing gold eyes and his lips curved in the briefest of smiles. Her response was a smile of relief and thanks.

It scared her how much she was beginning to depend on Theo Bradley.

★   ★   ★

Alicia moved back to the estate the next day.

Theo was impressed. 'She didn't hang around. I thought those arty types would take forever to accomplish anything.'

Rosie smiled and handed him the

file he'd requested. 'They move fast when they want to — look how quickly they've arranged tonight's party. Besides, Alicia's not like the rest of them. She's the sensible one.'

Theo doubted Alicia was as sensible as Rosie would have him believe, or she would have been keen to stay away from her ex-husband. Probably a good idea not to say so out loud.

'I think we should go to this party,' he said instead.

'Oh, no. I couldn't possibly stand it. It will be awful — there'll be too many people. It will be rough and noisy.'

'I'll be there to take care of you.' His look made her shiver.

'I don't need taking care of. It's just — that kind of thing's not my scene. Besides, if we go I'll have Evie whingeing. She's always desperate to go to these parties.'

He put the file down on the desk and sat back thoughtfully.

'We could take Evie.'

'I don't think so.'

'Why not?'

Rosie stood firm with hands on hips. 'Didn't you hear what I said? Wild crowds. Noise. There might even be fighting. It wouldn't be a suitable environment for a fifteen-year-old.'

'Have you ever been to any of these parties?'

'Don't be ridiculous. Of course I haven't.'

'Then how do you actually know the environment will be unsuitable?' He wasn't being awkward — he genuinely thought it would be a good idea to attend the party and he couldn't understand her reluctance. It would be a gentle introduction for him to the estate inhabitants. Besides, the prospect of another evening out with Rosie held a massive appeal.

'I know what they're like,' she argued.

'Okay, how about the three of us show our faces — just for an hour. We'll leave long before there's an opportunity for things to get out of hand. You know

I wouldn't suggest taking you or Evie into a danger zone.'

She was considering it, he was glad to see. 'Just an hour?'

'Definitely no more than an hour. They need to see me around the place. I don't want to make a big announcement — I'd rather slip quietly into estate life. And this will give me an opportunity to do just that. And for us to show we're a team.'

'Okay.' She was still reluctant, but at least she'd agreed. 'But only for an hour. And any sign of trouble . . . '

'We'll leave straight away.'

It was the music that hit them first — a wall of pure sound that reverberated through the airspace and assaulted them square in the face as they entered the old barn. Rosie tried not to smile as she noticed Theo reeling back.

'They like it loud,' she shouted by way of explanation. 'Come and sit and I'll fetch you a drink.'

She led the way to a table in the

corner — farthest away from the noisy speakers.

'I don't want to sit way back here,' Evie complained.

'You're lucky you're here at all,' Rosie countered and was relieved when Evie nodded her agreement.

'I know,' she admitted. 'But I'm going to have a word with Alicia to welcome her home before I'm forced to sit it out with you lot at the back like some hermit.'

Rosie smiled despite herself. Only Evie would have considered sitting in on this lively party as being in the least hermit-like. As far as Rosie was concerned, it was wild living.

She pushed her way to the makeshift bar, picking up a beer for Theo and a diet cola each for herself and Evie.

She'd had reservations about coming here tonight, but her sister had pleaded and coaxed. And when Theo had added his voice — pointing out it would be a good opportunity to present a united front — Rosie had eventually given in.

But they were only staying for a short while, only long enough to mark Alicia's return, and Rosie had made sure Evie understood that. She was lucky her sister was rarely a sulky teenager, even if she did like to argue her point. She'd accepted Rosie's final rulings with good grace and had agreed they would leave after a short while.

'Our darling Alicia is returned to us.' Marsha swooped as soon as Rosie returned to the table. 'Isn't it wonderful?'

Rosie smiled. 'Yes — it's terrific.'

'I was worried this day would never arrive. I've missed her so much.' With a satisfied smile, Marsha floated off — obviously pleased to have her friend and confidant back on the estate.

Rosie was pleased, too — Alicia was a lovely, serene presence and it was good to have her return to where she belonged. She was obviously keen to be here — her move back had happened so quickly after that initial phone call to Marsha. And now, only days later, friends and tenants had turned out to celebrate.

Theo leaned in and spoke in Rosie's ear. 'Don't you think it's weird?' She shivered as his warm breath tickled, but she couldn't object — it was so noisy it had been necessary.

Just as it was necessary for her to lean closer to speak to him, so close that she could smell him — all warm and clean and citrusy fresh — the kind of smell that seemed calculated to turn a girl's head.

'Do I think what's weird?'

'That Alicia would chose to come back to the place she was humiliated — the place her ex-husband lives.'

It was bound to seem odd to him — particularly as Alicia was now dancing energetically with Adam Powell as though they didn't have a shared, and not very pleasant, history.

'They didn't have a conventional marriage. None of them have — they call it love, but the way they behave is disgraceful. I think that's what's put me off relationships. I've seen how they carry on.' She couldn't keep the disgust from her voice.

Someone jostled their rickety old table. Theo put a hand out to steady it before their drinks went flying.

'You've never been in love?'

'Never have been, never will be,' she returned hotly. 'I'm too keen on self-preservation for such nonsense.'

Theo didn't say any more on the subject and she was glad. She'd said too much, revealed too much. In this noisy, crowded barn where they'd been forced closer just to be heard, the sense of intimacy had overwhelmed her.

There was a bit of a commotion as the remaining members of the band gathered on the area cleared for dancing, instruments in hand.

'What are they doing?'

Rosie sighed. 'I'm very much afraid that they're either going to fight or they're going to play.'

'It seems they're going to play,' he said as they heard the tuning of a guitar. 'Well, I wasn't expecting that.' He was silent for a minute and then the question anyone would have asked in the same situation burst forth. 'Who's going to sing?'

Rosie stifled a gasp. Of course he'd asked, why wouldn't he? It was the first thing anyone wanted to know whenever The Noise got together to play.

'George,' she replied flatly, as the youngster — looking more rock star than farmhand in his torn denims and leather jacket, his too-long hair down to his shoulders — took the mic and began to belt out one of the group's hits.

'He's good,' Theo commented. 'He's wasted on the farm.'

Rosie shrugged. 'I only hope he'll see sense and think of his own future before it's too late. The college won't hold his place open indefinitely.'

They didn't speak while the band played. Theo seemed to be listening intently, but Rosie was too preoccupied with her thoughts to take proper notice.

A dull ache in the region of her heart made her wish she hadn't come tonight. Times like this highlighted that her father was missing — he would have loved this, been in his element. Instead, George had taken his place, singing, strutting as though he was born to it. And, Rosie supposed, he had — he certainly had more right up there than any stranger. He'd been born on the road with the band and had grown up with them.

'I suppose there's no point waiting for the weekend to have a party when every day's a holiday,' Theo reflected as the band packed away after half a dozen songs, and the energetic dancing resumed once again.

'They don't need to work, they wrote the songs for The Noise — they still earn a fortune in royalties.'

'What happens to your father's share?'

'Harry,' was the one-word answer.

11

Theo was aware of Rosie frantically scanning the noisy barn.

'What is it?' he asked.

'Have you seen Evie?' she demanded, still looking around. 'It's been a while since I saw her . . . '

'Dancing with George.' Theo nodded in the direction of the dance floor and he heard Rosie draw a sharp breath. 'What?'

'He's too old for her.'

'They're only dancing.'

'Yes, but look how . . . ' Rosie winced as Evie raised her arms around George's neck and the two of them began slow dancing in the middle of the pandemonium on the dance floor as everyone else threw themselves around to an upbeat number.

Rosie needed to be distracted. Perhaps, if she learned to have a little fun herself, she might be a bit more understanding about Evie's behaviour.

'Dance with me?' he invited, holding out his hand, but Rosie shook her head

'Not here, it wouldn't be seemly,' she told him primly. 'I'm in charge, the estate manager. I don't want to make a spectacle of myself.'

'And I'm the estate owner, but I don't have a problem with dancing,' he said.

She didn't like that — he could see it in the way her green eyes narrowed and her full lips settled into an unyielding line.

'I'm not pulling rank, Rosie. Just suggesting we might enjoy finishing that dance we started at Chudley House.'

He felt her shudder at the suggestion. 'That would cause gossip. And I don't like being talked about.'

He sighed. Her upbringing really had done a proper job of bundling her up tight, her realised. Trying a different tack, he observed, 'I think these people are far too self-absorbed to give a second thought to anyone else. I mean, have any of them even asked you what I'm doing here?'

He knew he'd hit home when she paled, but he felt no satisfaction. She pushed back from the table and got to her feet.

'I have to get Evie out of here — apart from anything else, it's a school night.'

'It's only ten, a few more minutes won't do any harm. Let her enjoy herself a little while longer.'

As he spoke, he could see a look of horror sweeping over Rosie's face and he glanced over in time to see George lowering his head until his lips were on Evie's.

'She's fifteen,' Theo reminded her as he got to his own feet and took her hand. 'It's only to be expected that she might have an interest in boys.'

'I have to put a stop to this . . . ' She took a couple of steps and stopped as Theo tightened his hold of her hand.

'Don't, Rosie. Let's get some air.' He

led her towards the door and she cast one last glance over her shoulder before they went outside. The base from inside the barn thumped against the chilly night air and Rosie shivered. Ever the gentleman, Theo shrugged out of his jacket and draped it over her shoulders.

'Thanks, but there's no need.'

'Rosie, will you stop arguing for just a minute . . . '

'Why did you pull me out of there? I don't like leaving her, not with George all over her.'

'She's a sensible girl and George is a nice boy. Besides, if you make a fuss you'll blow the whole thing out of proportion and force them closer. You have to trust her.'

She looked up at him, her green eyes filled with anxiety, and Theo wanted to gather her up in his arms and promise her everything would be fine. Instead, he decided to make sure she was okay after the band's impromptu performance.

'It must be odd seeing someone else

taking your dad's place — singing the songs he was famous for.'

'It's really the only time I miss him,' she admitted. 'He was never around much, any other time.'

Again, Theo wanted to gather her up and take care of her. It was most odd. 'Tonight's rough on you. I can see that.'

She gave a brief shrug. 'I'm more worried about Evie just now,' she admitted.

'And I'm worried about you. If you tried to relax, stopped taking the cares of the world on your shoulders, you might start to enjoy yourself.'

She shivered again, despite the warmth of his jacket. Or maybe it was because of the jacket — she could smell his cologne on it and it was as though he'd wrapped her in a hug.

'How can I relax and stop worrying? My sister's being mauled by a hormonal teenager and you want to be a comedian. This isn't a time for jokes.'

He regarded her with burning golden eyes and she could feel herself melt, yield unwillingly to his iron will. 'It's not a joke. I'm deadly serious. You need to think of yourself occasionally.'

'You might be my employer, but how can you possibly think you can tell me what to do on a personal level?'

His gaze was unflinching. 'Because you'll make a better job of managing the estate if you're happy.' He grinned and her stomach flipped. Damn him — how could he make her react like this even when she was desperate to resist him? Quite apart from her own feelings, he was her boss. This was most inconvenient.

'I *am* happy,' she insisted. And for a moment, as she looked into his eyes, it was true.

She watched as he ran a hand roughly though his black as night hair. 'Okay, Rosie Farnham.' He laughed softly. 'But one of these days you're going to let go. And I very much hope I'm around when it finally happens.'

Needing to get away, she shrugged his jacket from her shoulders and handed it back to him. 'I'd better go back inside and fetch Evie.'

And she walked away. Even though she wanted to stay.

★ ★ ★

'You do need to have fun — I think Theo has a point.' Julia took a rather delicious-looking home-made carrot cake from her fridge, cut two very generous slices and placed them on plates. 'Here.' She handed one to Rosie.

'I know you do.' She had wondered whether or not she should confide in her friend; it seemed disloyal to Theo, somehow. But, she and Julia were close and Rosie knew it would go no further. 'This cake is delicious.'

'Thanks, I found the recipe online. And I can't believe you didn't take the opportunity to have some fun with Theo Bradley.'

Rosie paused, fork midway to her mouth. 'Why would I have done that?'

'Oh, I don't know. Perhaps because

he's sinfully gorgeous and he seems to care about you.'

'He barely knows me.'

'But he obviously likes what he does know. Seems it all went on last night. I almost wish I'd gone to that party now.'

'Yes — why didn't you?' Rosie latched onto the change in subject and ran with it.

'That lot are a bit too wild for my liking, thank you very much. I'm surprised you went, you don't normally go to those things.'

'We didn't stay long. Theo thought it was a good idea for us to show our faces. And Evie was keen to go.'

Julia was silent for a moment. 'You took Evie?'

'Just for an hour or so. Only now I wish I hadn't — she seems to have developed a growing attachment to George.'

Rosie squirmed under the glare of Julia's disapproval. Julia could really be quite straight-laced sometimes. Rosie knew there was no way she would have allowed Louise to go to the party. She felt ever so slightly guilty — perhaps she should have insisted on staying at home last night. It would have saved a whole lot of problems.

Julia tucked her hair behind her ear. 'But George is eighteen. He's too old for her.'

'That's what I said.' Rosie sighed. 'But what can I do? As Theo pointed out, if I lay the law down he'll only seem more attractive to her.'

'If you're worried, you should forbid her to see him. Three years is a big difference at her age. Theo might be gorgeous, but be honest, what does he know about teenage romances?'

'More than us, obviously, because he's right. However much I don't like the situation, I'm going to have to sit tight and hope it fizzles out.'

'There must be some way you can put a stop to it.'

'Not that I can think of.' Rosie sighed. 'And it could be worse — she could have taken up with someone who rode a motorbike and I'd have to worry in case she rode on the back of it.'

'I suppose so. I don't like it, though.' Julia sighed heavily and then tucked into her cake.

Rosie frowned. She couldn't help but wonder why Julia took such a great interest in the way Rosie raised Evie. Whatever the problem or decision, Julia was always forceful in her opinions. Rosie supposed it was the kind of advice close friends offered and she was grateful for the support, so she really shouldn't be questioning Julia's motives. Best to change the subject.

'This frosting is heavenly! It's like eating a soft, sweet cloud.'

'Thank you — it's cream cheese. I don't think we're ever going to agree about Theo,' Julia admitted. 'You've proved you can manage without a man — but just because you can doesn't mean you have to.'

Rosie bit back a smile. Since Julia had married Bob and become step-mother to Louise, she'd been preaching the joys of marriage and family life to anyone who'd listen.

'Not everyone is as happily married as you and Bob, you know. Besides, Theo just said I should relax and have fun. He didn't suggest that fun should be with him.'

'Of course he meant for you to have fun with him. And you never know, a bit of fun can lead to something serious once in a while. Besides, you can't let the lifestyle your father chose jeopardise your future happiness.'

Rosie bristled defensively. 'This has nothing to do with Dad. I'm doing fine on my own.'

Julia smiled indulgently. 'One of these days, I hope you fall in love and you won't know what's hit you.'

Rosie shook her head. 'Never going to happen. Now, can we change the subject?'

'Oh, all right. How are plans going for the move?'

Rosie grimaced. She still wasn't happy at having to move into Farnham

House, but Theo wouldn't entertain the alternative of them staying at the manor.

'Theo's arranged for an army of people to redecorate the place. They should be done by the end of next week.'

'It's amazing what money can do,' Julia commented wistfully. 'Bob and I have been trying to get someone to come in and decorate our living room for months.'

'I was kind of hoping it would take ages to sort the house out. I'm not keen on leaving the manor.'

'I know, honey.' Julie patted her hand. 'But that old manor's been nothing but trouble. You can have a fresh start and you won't be beholden to Harry for anything.'

That was true. Instead she was going to be dependent on Theo's goodwill. Somehow that didn't scare her half as much as it should have.

* * *

Theo was looking for Rosie. He seemed to spend his life looking for Rosie, these days. And oddly, he didn't seem to mind.

He found Evie in the kitchen. 'Any idea where your sister is?'

At first he thought he was seeing things. He blinked. Twice. He'd had no inkling any of Evie's donkeys were domesticated.

'At Julia's. She won't be long.' Evie poured herself a glass of orange juice and replaced the carton in the fridge. It seemed, as far as she was concerned, that there was nothing amiss.

His initial instinct had been to say nothing, but curiosity got the better of him. 'Evie, why is there a donkey in your kitchen? And why is she eating an apple from the fruit bowl?'

'This is Jessie,' Evie told him solemnly, stroking the little donkey's grey fur. 'She's been my best friend, like, forever.'

'I thought Louise was your best friend.'

Evie's eyes narrowed. 'You know what I mean,' she told him.

He supposed he did. Animal companions were supposed to be very comforting — although he'd never been able to see the attraction himself.

'She likes to go for walks, so I often bring her down here.'

He raised an eyebrow. 'What does Rosie say about that?'

Evie laughed. 'Okay, correction. I often bring her down here when Rosie's out.'

Theo smiled. He'd thought as much. 'You said she wasn't going to be long.' He glanced out of the window. 'In fact — isn't that her now, walking towards the manor?'

Evie raced over to the window. 'Oh, no. We have to get Jessie out. Quick, help me. Rosie will go bananas if she catches her in the house. I promised last time it wouldn't happen again.'

Theo stifled a smile. 'I think it's a bit late now.'

Rosie was talking into her mobile as

she came through the door. 'I'll be there as soon as I can . . . Yes, Miss Morris, very inconvenient, I understand that . . . Okay, I'll see you in a minute.'

'What's wrong?' Evie asked.

'Your donkeys are out.' Rosie's face was a picture of dismay. 'Running wild all over the village.'

'Oh, no.'

'Yes. Oh, no.' Rosie put her hands on her hips and Theo braced himself for shouting. But at least it wouldn't be directed at him. 'And what is Jessie doing inside — again? I've told you before, donkeys are not indoor animals.'

'I was just about to take her back to the sanctuary,' Evie replied contritely.

'Too right you're taking her back. And stay with her until we find out how the others got out. There might be a gap in the fence somewhere. In the meantime, I'd best go and round up the escapees.'

'I'll give you a lift down to the village,' Theo offered.

The fact she was happy to go to the

village in his car told him how desperate she was to minimise inconvenience to the locals. They stopped briefly at the sanctuary so Rosie could collect the halters she would need to lead the animals back. While there, they easily spotted the weak spot in the fence where the animals had pushed through.

'It will be Mr Kennedy's fault,' Rosie decided. 'He'll be the ringleader in all this. He always frets when Jessie's not here. Evie knows that. He will have gone looking for her, and the others will have followed.'

This all made very little sense to Theo. 'Why would Mr Kennedy have gone looking for Jessie when there were other donkeys in the field to keep him company?'

Rosie sighed and got back in with the halters. 'He's in love.'

This was just bizarre. 'Do donkeys fall in love? Really?'

'Don't laugh,' Rosie scolded. 'You only have to see the two of them together to see — he follows her everywhere.'

On the way, she called George, asking him to have a look at the fence. And, as they drove into the village, Miss Morris was waiting for them.

'It's pandemonium!' she shrieked. 'I've even had to shut the shop to keep an eye on them. Running wild, they were.'

Theo glanced over at the four donkeys peacefully grazing on the village green and felt the urge to laugh.

'I'm so sorry you were inconvenienced,' Rosie told her. 'And thank you for letting me know. Evie was due to check on them shortly and we'd have been worried when they weren't there.'

'Glad I was able to help. If I hadn't spotted them, anything could have happened.' Miss Morris was in her element as the one who had averted certain disaster.

'What could have happened to them?' Theo asked in an urgent whisper as Miss Morris returned to reopen her shop.

Rosie smiled. 'Probably not much. They would have stayed here grazing for most of the afternoon. Of course, if they'd wandered back onto the road it might have been different.'

She slipped a halter onto the nearest donkey. 'Okay, Mr Kennedy, old boy,' she told him soothingly. 'Let's see if we can get you back to your girlfriend.'

'I'll walk with you. I'll come back for my car later.'

It didn't take long to lead the donkeys back to the sanctuary. Evie was already there with Jessie. George was working to repair the damage to the fence. As though to prove Rosie was right, Mr Kennedy broke free and trotted over to where the little grey donkey was rolling happily in the grass.

Rosie looked over her shoulder and grinned. 'What did I tell you? He's a donkey in love.'

Theo grinned back, feeling quite sorry for poor old Mr Kennedy — and very grateful that he had guarded his own heart against such foolishness.

12

They had all been right. Rosie hated to admit it, but she loved the new house as soon as she and Evie moved in. It was properly insulated, watertight, light and airy. Everything the manor wasn't. And it was less than half the size, so there would be less to clean. If she hadn't been so stubborn, so adamantly preoccupied with the history of the place, she and Evie might have moved to live in some comfort years ago.

'Well?' Theo demanded as he dumped down a box of kitchen equipment noisily on the counter. 'What do you think of it?'

'It's — okay.' The admission was grudging. Rosie didn't like being wrong — even when it meant a better outcome for her.

He grinned and — she couldn't help it — the corners of her mouth tugged and before she knew it, she was smiling back.

'Fine; you were right and I was wrong. I love it. Evie loves it, too. We should have moved years ago.'

She expected him to say he'd told her so and was pleasantly surprised when he didn't.

'Looks like you brought all your stuff over just in time.' He nodded towards the window. The wind had been high all day, making the move difficult and bringing down two trees that she knew of, but now heavy rain had been added into the mix.

Rosie shuddered, just imagining the state the manor would be in. Their rain buckets would be needed with bells on today.

'Sure you're going to be okay on your own at the manor?'

'Why?' Arms folded, he leaned back against the work surface and there was a mischievous gleam in his golden eyes. 'Do you want to offer me a bed here?'

She sighed. She was tempted. Very

tempted. But having him stay with her overnight wasn't the kind of example she wanted to set Evie. 'I don't like to think of you staying there while we're living in such luxury,' she confessed.

'So now you understand how I felt about you staying there. But yes, I'll be fine for tonight. I have to go back to London in the morning in any case.'

'Oh.' The disappointment took her by surprise. Since when had it been any of her business what Theo got up to? And it wasn't so long ago that she'd have celebrated his departure with an energetic jig. He'd very quickly become a fixture, and she was used to — and liked — having him around.

'There's a business merger at a delicate stage of operations and I have no choice — I have to be there.'

She nodded. Of course he did. He might have been playing at estates for the past while, but his real life lay miles away. She was just going to have to become used to his not being here.

The mobile in the pocket of her jeans

rang. 'Excuse me,' she told Theo as she fished it out.

It was Marsha — near hysterical as she cried down the phone. Rosie winced.

'Calm down, I can't understand what you're saying.'

'I tried to stop them, I really did. But George and his father just had the most awful argument. And they've run off into this terrible weather . . . '

'Who's run off? Victor and George?'

'No!' Marsha sobbed. 'George and Evie.'

'Evie? What was she doing with you?' As far as Rosie knew, she'd been at Louise's house, doing homework.

It was starting already, she realised, the sneaking around, the untruths, so she could spend time with George. How much worse would it be if she forbade her sister from seeing the boy? Theo had been right; she had no choice but to accept it. But for now, a more pressing matter superseded her annoyance that Evie had misled her. 'Where did they go, Marsha?'

'I don't know,' Marsha wailed down the line. 'I'm just so worried. The weather's so wild and the sky's so dark. And a tree's just blown down across the lane here. What if something falls on them?'

Rosie bit her lip. Marsha's tendency to over-dramatise every situation annoyed her, but she realised that maybe this time the drama was justified.

'I'm sure they'll be okay,' she muttered despite her own concerns. 'I'll try and call Evie and get back to you soon, Marsha. Try and stay calm.'

'What's wrong?' Theo asked as she frantically tried to press the tiny buttons on her mobile with shaking hands.

'George fell out with his father and stormed out of the house. And Evie's with him. I'm just going to phone, see if they're okay.'

Evie's mobile went straight to voice-mail.

'I can't get through.' Rosie's lips were numb. She had a bad feeling about this.

'Where do you think they've gone?'

She glanced towards the window again and shuddered. 'Probably the sanctuary, to make sure the donkeys are okay.' Rosie snatched her waterproof jacket from the chair she'd draped it over. 'I'm going to go and see if I can find them.'

'I'll go,' Theo offered. 'You should stay here in case they come back.'

'I can't just sit here like a lemon!' She zipped her jacket up as she hurried to the door.

He caught up with her in two strides. His hand closed around her upper arm and she could have sworn she felt the warmth of his fingers through her jacket.

'Rosie, be sensible. You had trouble walking in here from the car, and the wind's much stronger now.'

'But you think you'll be okay in it?'

'Given that I'm much bigger and heavier than you are, yes.'

She tried and failed to pull her arm out of his grasp and realised she was dealing with six foot four of solid muscle. Yes, he was stronger and bigger — that probably meant he'd be able to cover more ground than she would in this weather.

'Oh, okay — but if you're not back in ten minutes I'm coming after you.'

'Make it fifteen.' He opened the door, letting the wind howl into the kitchen, and stepped out into the storm, head down, collar pulled up. And then he was gone.

She realised her mistake as soon as the door crashed closed against the gale — now she was going to be worried about him, too. She paced nervously, tempted to go after him, but knowing that what he'd said made sense. Not only had she found it near impossible to breathe out there, but she'd nearly been lifted off her feet earlier, despite heavy boxes weighing her down.

* * *

Theo made his way to the sanctuary, the wind howling and blowing debris all around him. He wondered in exasperation whether Rosie ever did anything without arguing, but to be fair, she'd been running her own show so long that she probably found it difficult to listen to advice. He was glad she'd agreed to stay at home, though — he didn't like the thought of her being buffeted around by this gale. She was so tiny, she wouldn't have stood a chance.

His hair was wet through, rainwater running freely down his face, by the time he spotted the teenagers. They were outside the donkeys' barn, both sitting on the rain-soaked ground, and it looked as though Evie had . . . Heart pounding, he put his head down against the wind and broke into as fast a run as the weather allowed.

'What happened?' He had to shout to be heard.

'A branch fell and hit her.' George was pale and on his knees next to a dazed Evie. 'We didn't see it coming.'

'Are you okay, Evie?' Wetness seeped through the knees of his jeans from the soft ground as he knelt down to get a better look at Evie's injury. 'That looks like a nasty gash on your forehead,' he said gently.

'I'm fine, thanks,' Evie muttered, still looking a little dazed.

'Does it hurt anywhere?' He was trying to establish how badly she was injured, working out if they would need specialist medical equipment, such as a backboard and collar, before she could be moved.

'Only my head. It just hit my head.' It seemed she hadn't suffered a neck or back injury, which was something.

Theo turned his attention to George. 'Did she lose consciousness at any point?'

'I don't know — maybe for a minute. She was knocked off her feet, it's a big branch.' George waved in the direction of what looked like half a tree lying in the barnyard.

The wind continued to whip itself up into a frenzy around them. Theo wanted to shout at George for being so uncertain and for his stupidity in endangering Evie by bringing her out in this storm. But he deemed it more important at this point to get Evie out of the wind and rain, and to somewhere where her wound could be attended to.

'What are you doing?' George asked as Theo swept Evie into his arms.

'She's not in any fit state to walk.'

'I'm fine,' Evie argued.

'No you're not,' Theo insisted. 'Besides, you barely weigh more than a feather, in this wind you'd find it hard going even without the injury. This is the quickest way to get us out of here.' She was bigger than Rosie, but even so, Theo barely registered her weight in his arms. He braced himself against the wind and headed back in the direction of Rosie's new home.

She was watching at the window and came running out into the driving rain as soon as she saw them.

'What's happened?' she yelled over the noise of the wind.

'Nothing to worry about.' Theo down-played the situation, despite knowing a head injury was always cause for concern. 'She's just had a little accident.'

'There's blood. Evie, your forehead's bleeding and your face is covered in scratches.'

'I'm fine,' Evie protested. 'Thanks for the lift, Theo, but you can put me down now.'

Theo obliged and set her on her feet on the gravel driveway, near his car. The teenager swayed uncertainly.

'We're going to hospital,' he informed them mildly. 'Just to have Evie's wound cleaned up and looked at.'

'There's no need. A bath and a rest and I'll be good as new.'

'Stop arguing,' Rosie snapped. 'We need to have a doctor look at you.'

'No way. I don't want any fuss and I'm not going near any doctor,' she said stubbornly.

'Evie, be reasonable,' Rosie pleaded.

'I'm fifteen — old enough to decide if

I need medical attention,' she added defiantly.

If the situation hadn't been so concerning, Theo might have laughed. Rosie was getting a taste of her own stubbornness. In contrast to her beautiful sister, however, the younger Farnham was likely to respond to his charm — a fact he intended to use to his advantage now.

'Evie, it's obvious you're fine, but you suffered a bit of a blow to the head and I'd feel happier if you allowed a doctor to examine you.'

'Oh, all right then.' Evie nodded and winced. 'Ouch.'

He was aware of Rosie at his side, rolling her eyes heavenward, and he paused just long enough to grin at her before unlocking the car and bundling them all in.

Rosie sat in the front with Theo while George kept a close eye on Evie in the back. In all likelihood, she was fine — certainly if her backchat was any indication. But Rosie was glad Theo had convinced her to go for a check-up.

Not that she would ever have admitted it out loud, but she was incredibly impressed — not only that he'd talked Evie into seeing a doctor, but that he'd allowed them all into his car — mud and all. The pristine leather interior was now covered in dirt, and he hadn't so much as given it a second glance. And she knew how much he loved his car.

The journey took forever. There were trees down everywhere — and debris strewn across every road that made Rosie fancy the place looked as though it had been through an apocalypse.

But eventually they drove into the hospital grounds and Evie was being helped out of the car and into the building.

★   ★   ★

'I didn't think they'd keep her in.' Rosie looked pale and exhausted as they drove through the gates of the Farnham Manor Estate, several hours later.

'As the doctor told you, it's just a

precaution.' Theo manoeuvred his car along the driveway for a short while before taking a sharp left turn to go down to the cottages inhabited by the old rockers. He glanced in his rear view mirror at George. 'Which one is it?'

George had been subdued all the way back. It was obvious that he was just as worried about Evie as Rosie was.

'Second one along.'

Theo kept the engine running but turned in his seat to speak to the teenager. 'Do you want us to come in with you?'

'Thanks, but it's probably best if I go in on my own. Perhaps you could have a word with them tomorrow, though. They might listen to you.'

Theo somehow doubted George's neurotic parents would listen to anyone, but he'd promised he'd try. The situation had gone on too long — and they had to be encouraged to see the impact they were making on their son's life.

'What was that about?' Rosie asked after George had disappeared into the cottage he shared with his parents.

Theo put the car in gear and effected a three-point turn in the narrow lane. 'George asked for my help in trying to persuade his parents to take responsibility for themselves. He really wants to take up that college place.' He felt rather than heard Rosie's soft sigh. 'What is it?'

'They've started to come to you for help. They already see you as their protector.'

'Is that a bad thing? If it takes the pressure off you . . . '

She sighed again, louder this time. 'You're right. I never realised what a burden it was, being responsible for so many adults who should be taking care of themselves.'

They pulled up at the house and sat for a moment. The wind had died down now, but they were both reluctant to venture out into the rain.

'Shall we make a dash for it?' Rosie asked at last.

Theo felt a jolt of welcome surprise.

'You're asking me in?'

'I can't expect the hero of the hour to make his own supper at this time of night.' Before he could reply, she tumbled out of the car and ran, head down, towards the back door.

Theo followed without a moment's hesitation.

* * *

The kitchen was warm and cosy and Rosie busied herself with preparing supper. Theo glanced over from his seat at the kitchen table, to where she was toasting sandwiches on the Aga. She still looked tired and pale. Not surprising after the day she'd had — moving home was supposed to be one of the most stressful events in life and she'd had the drama with Evie to contend with, too. As his gaze clashed with weary green eyes, the urge to protect her had never been stronger.

'Can I help you with that?'

He'd always guarded his heart by

being a loner, but he realised he actually wanted to spend time with Rosie. Wanted to share even mundane tasks, such as preparing supper. He suspected he should be worried. But he wasn't.

'Thanks, but I think I can handle a couple of toasties.' Her smile softened the refusal. 'But you can talk to me.'

'What do you want to talk about?'

Deftly she flipped the sandwiches over. 'Your family.'

'You've met him.'

'Lysander? But surely it's not just the two of you. What about your parents? Where are they?'

'Dead.'

'Both of them?'

'Yes.'

'I'm sorry.' She brought the sandwiches over and sat down opposite him.

'Thank you.' He reached across the table and took her hand. She liked the feel of his fingers wrapped around hers and looked up to find the gold of his eyes had darkened.

She couldn't have a fling with him as Julia and Evie had suggested — as she was tempted to do — she wasn't made that way. But in the short time she'd known him, she'd grown to trust him, to think of him as a friend.

She held his gaze. Unlike the other males who had littered her life, Theo was someone who had proved he could be trusted. Nobody else she knew would have battled through such foul weather to rescue her sister.

And nobody else would still be here to hold her hand.

13

'Keep your coat on, we're going out.' Theo was being deliciously masterful this morning as Rosie arrived at the manor and let herself into the estate office.

'I don't want to go too far in case Evie needs me. Besides, don't you have a meeting to go to?'

'I've postponed my meeting. And you've just dropped Evie at Julia's, where she's being extremely well looked after.' Theo logged off his laptop and got to his feet.

Rosie wondered briefly where they were going, but there was a more pressing matter on her mind. 'I was surprised Evie wanted to go to Julia's. I mean, she's only just out of hospital.'

'Evie's not in any danger and it makes sense for her to stay somewhere she can be mollycoddled. You're busy trying to settle into a new home and run an estate.'

'I suppose.' Her agreement was grudging — she should be the one fussing over her sister. She was family. Louise, Julia and Bob were only friends.

'What's happening with the donkeys?'

Rosie smiled. Even with a head injury, Evie had been thinking of the sanctuary. 'She's got George overseeing her volunteers for the next few days. He's snowed under, helping with the cleanup of the estate after yesterday, but he was keen to do something to help Evie. Why did you postpone your meeting? I thought you were needed.'

'I thought you might need me more.'

Her lips rounded into a silent 'oh'. Nobody had ever put her first before. She didn't quite know how to react.

'Tell me more about Julia,' he urged. 'She always seems very keen to have Evie. Is she related to you in any way?'

'No, just a friend. Why do you ask?' She tried to make it sound casual, but it

was odd he should ask about that —
after her own recent thoughts.

His lips parted, as though he was
about to say something, but then he
gave a brief shake of his head. 'It's just
that you seem very close.'

'She's been my best friend for five
years. She moved to the village just
after Dad died.'

'And you hit it off instantly?'

Rosie nodded. 'It was a huge shock
when I found Dad hadn't left any
provision in his will for Evie. Julia
listened as I whinged to my heart's
content — she was a godsend. She's
been a really good friend over the
years.'

'And she doesn't have any children of
her own?'

'She has Louise.'

'Her stepdaughter?'

'That's right. It works out really well
because the girls are close friends, too.'

He nodded, although she suspected
he understood very little about the true
value of female friendships.

'So, are you coming with me or not?' Theo's tone was one of infinite patience as he folded his arms and perched on the edge of the desk.

'That depends. Where are you going?' Rosie looked defiantly up. Despite the fact that he was gorgeous as sin this morning in black sweater and jeans, she had no intention of being pushed around.

'Shopping.'

'We have plenty of food.'

'Not that kind of shopping.'

Rosie didn't like the sound of that. 'I don't want to. I don't like shopping.'

His lips curved into a smile. 'A trip into town, that's all I'm suggesting. It will be quick and painless — I promise.'

*   *   *

Rosie was uneasy as she sat in Theo's helicopter, headphones at the ready and belt buckled. Her first experience of flying — she should have been enjoying it. Instead, she sat, a bundle of nerves, worried about her sister and staring, unseeingly, out of the window at the world far below. It was a beautiful day, sun shining and not a single cloud to be seen — it was hard to believe it was the same world as yesterday when it had been so wild.

Theo had summoned the helicopter with nothing more than a brief phone call — the pilot had been on standby and had arrived within minutes. This was luxury beyond her comprehension. Beyond anything she ever expected or wanted.

'I've never before known a woman be so miserable when I've offered to take her shopping.' Theo sounded genuinely perplexed as his voice reached her through the earphones.

'Then I don't think I want to meet the kind of women you normally associate with.'

'We're only going to visit a handful of shops. You need some new clothes. Much as you look edible in those worn jeans, I'd like my estate manager to have a few smart items in her wardrobe. And a couple of evening dresses for when you accompany me to functions.'

'What? Attending functions was never in the job description.'

'Would it have stopped you applying for the job if it had been?' he asked with a grin.

Of course it wouldn't. But she wasn't inclined to tell him that.

'I'd have thought twice.'

He laughed softly, the sound teasing her ears through the headphones. 'Liar.'

She flushed. 'Why would I want to accompany you to functions anyway?'

'Perhaps because of this mind-blowing, out-of-this-world, once-in-a-lifetime attraction we both feel.'

She felt her face flush. He was right, she couldn't deny it. Even now his voice made her heart beat faster.

'We've only just met.'

'It seems like I've known you all my life.'

'Cliché king,' she accused. 'If I could

afford it I'd insist on buying the new clothes myself.'

'I'd be grossly offended if you tried to pull a stunt like that.'

'I'm grossly offended that you seem to think you can order me around.'

He glanced over, and she saw his lips twitch. Despite her best efforts, she found herself smiling back before making a conscious effort to change the subject.

'When are you going to speak to Marsha and Victor?'

'Already have.'

She was impressed, if surprised. 'When did you find time?'

'I popped by this morning.'

'Surely they weren't up?' There was no way George's ageing rocker parents would be out of bed, even now.

'I don't think it was a case of them having risen — more a case of not having been to bed yet.'

She nodded — that was more likely. 'Did you get any sense out of them?'

'They don't want to live like that any

more. They know they're ruining George's chances of a decent future. And yesterday gave them a jolt. They've agreed they won't object to his leaving for college any longer.'

She glanced out of the tiny window at the world so far below, but the panoramic view was wasted on her preoccupied mind.

'That's good news. Very good news.'

She was quietly very impressed. That was more progress than she'd managed in all the years she'd been in charge. But then, she supposed, they were used to her. Theo had authority because he was new to the estate.

She smiled to herself. More likely Theo had authority because his very presence demanded it.

'So, happy with the house now you've spent a night there?'

She smiled. She might as well go for it — allow him to bask in his well-earned triumph. 'I know I resisted the move, but you were right about the manor. It's far too big and far too draughty. The house is much more cosy.'

'And it's nice to be cosy.'

She glanced at him through narrowed eyes. He was flirting, which she guessed was no big deal to him. She wasn't tempted however to flirt back. 'It's more than adequate for me and Evie.'

'And you're sure you'll be happy there? Once the manor's properly renovated, it's going to be spectacular.'

'I know.' She smiled softly. 'But Evie's happy as long as we're close enough to the sanctuary. And she doesn't seem to be expecting her mother to turn up any longer.'

Rosie's brow furrowed. She still couldn't understand why her sister had suddenly given up on Glory. Maybe it was just too many years filled with too many disappointments.

* * *

It was humiliating, the way Theo insisted on taking her to a succession of

217

designer boutiques — and the way he footed the bills for the ultimate fantasy wardrobe. Someone else's fantasy, she hastened to tell herself — she was much too busy and sensible to worry about clothes. And even if she hadn't been, no way would she have wanted a man to buy clothes for her. She had tried to tell Theo as much as he had dragged her through the door of the first establishment.

'I'm earning a decent wage now. Once I'm on my feet, I'll be able to buy my own clothes.'

'You obviously haven't thought through the full implication of our agreement.'

'What do you mean?'

'Part of the job,' he told her, 'is to look the part. You need to be adequately and expensively dressed, otherwise my judgement will be called into question — people will start to wonder why I've employed you. Just think of the clothes as your uniform for the job and you'll be fine.'

Rosie felt suddenly sick. 'What have I

let myself in for?'

He grinned then and her stomach flipped. 'It will be worth it.' He smiled. 'I promise.'

* * *

Theo had only been able to postpone his meetings for twenty-four hours. He had no choice but to leave the next day. But he didn't want to go. In a short space of time, Rosie and the inhabitants of the estate had worked their way into his psyche and he felt he belonged here.

'How long will you be away?' Her face was devoid of emotion and Theo wondered what she was feeling. Was she pleased to have the place to herself again? He couldn't forget how desperate she'd been for him to leave that first day. Her expression gave nothing away — he didn't want to ask if she'd miss him, in case her answer wasn't what he wanted to hear.

'A couple of weeks at least. I've got some people doing the groundwork, but the merger isn't something I can delegate.'

He wanted to tell her he'd miss her, but resisted the urge. Regardless of whether she reciprocated, it would make him too vulnerable. He wanted to deny the admission, even to himself. Theo never missed anyone — and he was keen to keep it that way. But then the feisty Rosie Farnham wasn't just anyone.

'Well, I've got plenty to be going on with here.'

So she was sticking to business. 'Good.'

She nodded. 'I'll have all manner of people calling about the renovations, never mind the usual day-to-day stuff . . .'

Okay, enough. It was time to show her what she really meant to him, just once before he left.

'Rosie . . . shut up.' His words were softly spoken, but the look of surprise was exactly what he'd aimed for. He acted quickly, crossing the distance between them in two short strides. His hands fitted perfectly around her waist.

'What are you doing?' Was it his imagination, or was she breathless?

He lifted her effortlessly, so her eyes were level with his — eyes so green he could drown in them.

'This,' he explained as he slowly — so slowly, heightening anticipation yet giving her every chance to object — closed the space between them.

The kiss was everything he'd expected it to be. Leaving her was going to be harder than he'd thought.

14

With Theo away, time slowed to a standstill for Rosie. And yet, she'd never been busier. With plans for the estate to make and oversee, she didn't stop from the moment she got up until the minute her head hit the pillow. Even so, she still found it hard to sleep.

Evie, with her wound healing nicely, was spending more and more time with Louise over at Julia and Bob's house. Studying, she said. So how could Rosie object? But with her sister and Theo away, she'd never felt more alone.

'You're looking tired,' Julia told her over a quick cup of coffee when Rosie managed to grab five minutes.

'Thanks!' She sipped her drink and sank deeper into the sofa. She was tired. And so comfortable and cosy in the sitting room of her new home. Really, if Julia wasn't here it would be so easy to close her eyes and drift off to sleep right here. Although she knew she'd be wide awake at bedtime.

'I'm worried about you.' Julia leaned forward in her chair and put her cup down on the coffee table.

Rosie smiled in a way she hoped would convey there was no cause for concern. 'You worry too much.'

'If you moved things along with Theo, I'd worry less. You should be dating, enjoying getting to know each other.'

Suddenly, Rosie's coffee cup was the most interesting thing in the world. Anything rather than meet Julia's keen gaze.

'Things are fine as they are.'

Julia was quiet for a moment, seeming to consider Rosie's words. And then she smiled. 'Well, that's all right, then.'

'Are you sure you don't mind having Evie? I can't understand why she doesn't want to come home.'

'She's very welcome to stay as long as

she likes,' Julia assured her. 'It makes sense, you have enough going on here without taking care of an injured teenager. Now, what's this I hear about Evie calling Harry?'

Rosie pressed her lips together tightly. She hadn't been too impressed with that particular trick her little sister had pulled.

'You know Evie — family is important to her. She phoned to let him know we'd moved, and asked him to visit.'

Julia looked as outraged as Rosie still felt. 'Why would she do something like that?'

'She really wants to see him. Hopes the news will bring him out of the woodwork.'

'Even after all he's done?'

'Unfortunately, yes. I, of course, am hoping it ensures he never comes near the place.'

If he did, he would find Rosie still hadn't forgiven him for selling the manor from under her — even if his actions had brought Theo into their lives.

⋆   ⋆   ⋆

The conversation with Julia played on Rosie's mind for a long time after the other woman had left. Not the bit about Harry, but the bit about Theo. While she was still sure she wasn't interested in a relationship — permanent or otherwise — she remembered how gratefully she had leaned on him when Evie had been lost and injured. And how he was already sharing responsibility for the estate tenants. And, most of all, she remembered how she'd felt with his powerful arms around her and his lips kissing hers — she'd felt safe and cared-for.

She went to bed early each night, but sleep eluded her. Unwillingly she had to face the sorry fact that she missed him.

⋆   ⋆   ⋆

It was nearly a week later, while she was thumping her pillow in a fruitless attempt at finding a comfortable position, that she heard it. She sat up in bed. An unmistakable whirling sound.

Heart racing, she made it outside in time to see Theo's helicopter descend onto the field behind the house. She blinked, sure she was hallucinating. But there he was, appearing from the craft.

Mildly she registered surprise that the noise hadn't summoned Evie from Julia's house. Then she realised she might not have known what it was.

She watched Theo dip his dark head as he negotiated the rotor blades and made his way towards where she shivered at the edge of the field. The helicopter took off in a whirl of noise and lights, whipping up a breeze that had her hanging on to her oversized nightshirt with one hand and her hair with the other.

'What are you doing back? I wasn't expecting to see you.' Surprise had made her voice shrill, but he just grinned, all white teeth and crinkly gold eyes, and she felt her insides melt.

'I missed you, too.' And without giving her time to react, he closed the space between them and swept her clean off the ground, with one arm under her knees and the other supporting her back. 'You shouldn't have run over the gravel in bare feet.'

'I was curious to see who was showing off by turning up in a helicopter.' She was doing her best not to allow herself to relax against him. It felt startlingly good to be back in his arms. Her nostrils twitched as they were assailed by his achingly familiar masculine scent and suddenly, even breathing proved a challenge.

'Who did you think it would be?'

'Someone with more money than sense.' She shifted against him and was reminded how closely he was holding her. 'Put me down, Theo. This is ridiculous.'

'No more ridiculous than running out of the house half-dressed with no shoes on.' He carried her towards the house, over the gravel driveway and indoors, where he took the stairs two at a time. He wasn't even slightly out of breath when he kicked open her bedroom door and threw her down onto the sheets. She yelped a token protest when he threw off his jacket, kicked off his shoes and joined her on the bed.

'I've had one hell of a week. Takeover went bad — but we seem to have contained the situation.' He loosened his tie, undid the top button of his crisp white shirt and reached out for her, pulling her close against him until the heat from his body enveloped her.

'What are you doing?' She made a feeble attempt to pull away, but he was holding her tight. Then she realised that further protests would be useless — Theo's breathing told her he was already fast asleep.

Giving into the inevitable, she snuggled up against him and closed her eyes. Knowing he was back gave her an odd sense of calm, and she slept almost at once.

★ ★ ★

Theo looked down at Rosie, curled up like a kitten and still fast asleep. He hadn't been able to stay away from her. Escaping the madness at his work and spending the night fast asleep in her arms had been worth the trouble of rearranging the Paris trip. And, even if he'd been too exhausted to even talk to her properly, just being close to her had been enough. He was energised and ready to conquer the world.

When he'd first woken, he'd thought for a minute he'd still been dreaming. When he'd realised he really was in her bed — still dressed and his clothes now crumpled beyond redemption — it had been torture to tear himself away to hit the shower. Sleeping next to her felt so right.

He still didn't 'do' love, of course.

But they had something better than that — an understanding that would benefit them both without the complications a love match entailed.

She looked like an angel this morning. Her hair lay in a knot of vibrant curls around her exquisite face. Her full mouth sent out a silent invitation and he couldn't resist. He sank to his knees by the bedside and gently brushed his lips against hers.

She responded by kissing him back, her eyes still closed tight. Reluctantly, he pulled away and watched as her eyes fluttered open, confusion clouding their green depths.

'I have to go. I'm flying back to London in a few minutes.'

'What time is it?'

'Six a.m.'

'Can't you stay for breakfast? You have to go straight away?'

'I'm afraid so. I have several meetings this morning. And I need to change into something a little less . . . ' he looked down at the trousers and shirt he'd slept in and grimaced, 'comfort-able.'

'You work too hard.' She reached out and stroked his cheek, her soft fingers meeting with the resistance of a day's growth of hair. He felt a muscle began to pulse merrily on his jaw.

'You need a shave.' And then she smiled at him and he felt the world tipping on its axis.

★ ★ ★

By the time Rosie was properly awake, Theo was long gone. It was almost as though his arrival had been a dream. It was only the fact she'd slept so well that proved he'd been there. She'd never slept so soundly in her life before.

Her rested state, however, wasn't enough to prepare her for the shock of the visitor who turned up later that morning.

'What are you doing here?' she demanded of the overweight and balding man who stood on the doorstep.

'Evie said you'd moved.'

She eyed her brother suspiciously. 'So? What's that to you?'

'Please don't be like that. Can I come in? I want to talk.'

Rosie, who would have cheerfully throttled him only weeks ago, now just wanted him gone. But he was still her brother. Part of the very tiny family she belonged to. Grudgingly, she let him into the sitting room.

'I'm not too impressed with you.'

'I know.' Harry sat down without invitation. But he looked pale and ill and Rosie, despite herself, found it very hard to go for the jugular as he deserved. 'I'm not impressed with myself, either, believe me.'

Rosie paced the floor in front of him. 'Why did you do it, Harry? Sell the estate and leave me and Evie homeless? And without telling us, too. We had no idea, until Theo turned up.'

Harry's eyes were downcast and Rosie stared at him accusingly. 'Not even a phone call to warn us, Harry.

And you didn't return any of my calls.'

'I didn't know what to say to you.'

'How about 'I'm sorry' for a start?'

Harry looked up at her and she softened a little. He really didn't look well at all, and she'd never seen him so contrite.

'I'm sorry.'

She gave a brief nod and waited for him to continue.

'Theo will have told you about my gambling problem?'

She nodded again.

'There were men after me, Rosie. I'd been losing badly and had no hope of paying up. If I hadn't sold the estate they would have come down here themselves — and I wouldn't trust them to be around you and Evie. They're not nice people.'

Rosie stopped pacing and rounded on him. 'Don't try to make out you saved us from a worse fate.'

Harry held up a hand in a gesture of surrender. 'I'm not, I promise. But how could I let them come here after you?'

'How could you let it happen, Harry? How could you get yourself into a position where you put Evie in danger? And how could you leave us homeless?'

Harry shifted uncomfortably under Rosie's furious gaze. 'Lysander said his brother wouldn't throw you out. And he was right. You're not homeless, are you?'

'Only because I threw myself on Theo's mercy. Begged him to give me a job and to let us stay on the estate. You knew how important it was to Evie, how much she wanted to stay here so Glory would know where to find her.'

As she glared at him, her older brother burst into tears.

'I know I'm weak,' he sobbed and Rosie, despite everything, felt a twinge of sympathy. 'I couldn't help myself. Before I knew it I was in so deep. I don't know what I would have done if Lysander hadn't stepped in to help.'

Rosie sat beside him on the sofa and was annoyed to find her arm snaking around him. But what else could she do? He threw himself on her shoulder and sobbed some more.

She didn't quite know what to do next — even though he was her brother, they'd never had a close relationship. She patted his arm awkwardly.

'Tell me, how did Lysander become involved?'

Harry sat up straight and took a tissue from his pocket before blowing his nose noisily. 'I met him at a poker game. We got on — made a good team. I've been staying with him.'

'Well, it's good you've got some support.' Although she'd have very much preferred Harry get that support from anyone other than Lysander. He might be Theo's brother, but she really hadn't liked the man. It was also highly suspicious that he'd paid so much of Theo's money to a friend.

'Harry!' The door crashed open and the shriek was deafening as Evie, back from Julia's as though guided by some sixth sense, threw herself towards her brother and enveloped him in a hug. 'I've missed you so much.'

Obligingly, Harry brightened up and returned the hug. 'Good to see you, Evie. How are you? What happened to your head?'

Evie sat up straight and put her hand to the healing injury.

'Long story. How long are you staying?'

He glanced hesitantly at Rosie. 'Not too long. I only came to wish you both well in your new home. Oh, and to give you this, Rosie.' He searched in the pocket of his tweed jacket and handed her an envelope.

She couldn't help reacting with suspicion. 'What is it?'

'Open it and find out,' Evie urged, impatient as ever. Rosie threw her a despairing glance.

Carefully she took the envelope and peered inside. She well remembered the last time a man had delivered an envelope from his pocket, and tried to quell her fear and suspicion. If it was something bad, Harry wouldn't have brought it in person. He was a complete coward where confrontation was concerned.

Rosie's eyes widened in shock as she examined the contents. 'It's a cheque.'

'That's all I've got left from the sale of the estate, after settling my debts.'

Evie got to her feet and walked around to peer over Rosie's shoulder. 'Oh-my-gosh. We're rich.'

'No, we're not,' returned Rosie. This was a very nice gesture from Harry — but if Lysander hadn't practically defrauded Theo's company, the estate wouldn't have realised half of what it had fetched. 'This money belongs to Theo.'

She was pleased Evie didn't disagree, but Harry pouted quietly on the sofa, obviously unhappy.

Then Evie, normally a master of deflecting trouble, plunged right into another area of controversy.

'So, Harry, why don't you come down to see us more often?'

Harry glanced helplessly at Rosie, who bit her lip. What could she do? Despite all that had gone on before, Harry was trying to be a decent brother now, she really felt he was, and it seemed Evie was trying to pick another fight.

'Are you doing anything about your gambling?' Rosie asked him practically. If he was to be allowed back into their lives, she had to know what steps he'd taken to overcome his problem.

Harry rubbed his bald head. 'I'm getting help — seeing a therapist. Giving you the rest of that money is my pledge that I'm not going to gamble again.'

'You're sure about that?'

'Oh, yes.' Harry nodded. 'Very sure. I'm going to have to be very careful and not put myself in the path of temptation, but Lysander's promised to help. It really shook me up, you know, losing the estate. And I can't tell you how terrible I feel for leaving you to fend for yourselves — and for all the years I relied on you to keep me in funds.'

As Rosie listened to him talk, she found herself beginning to believe him. At last, Harry was turning into the kind of brother she'd always hoped for. Someone who would stand beside her and Evie and be proud to be a part of their family.

'In that case . . . ' She paused and cleared her throat. 'Harry, you're very welcome to visit us here, whenever you're able.'

15

Theo was staring at her, and she could tell he wasn't amused. Rosie shrugged. 'You said yourself, Lysander shouldn't have paid so much for the estate.'

'That doesn't mean I'm going to take money from you.'

Gold eyes glared, but she refused to be intimidated.

'Theo, it's your money.'

'Why don't you look on it as the salary your brother should have paid you over the past year? Because the amount he's given you should just about cover that.'

Rosie sighed loudly. She was beginning to wish she hadn't come to Bradley's to stay with him for the weekend after all. He'd sent a car for her and Evie last night, and they'd been pleased of the chance of a break — so much so that Evie had happily left

George in charge of the sanctuary.

And what a break. Theo's suite at Bradley's Hotel in central London was the ultimate in luxury. When Rosie first saw it she'd cringed at the recollection of what he must have thought when he'd turned up at the manor.

But now Theo was being so . . . well . . . 'You're being stubborn.' She planted her hands firmly on her hips and tried to stare him down, but he wasn't having any of it.

'Said the pot to the kettle. You're not going to win this time, Rosie. I'm not taking your money.' His voice was soft and a smile tugged at the corner of his lips, but his eyes were unrelenting and she knew he had no intention of giving in.

'I'll just have to buy you a very expensive present, then.'

Because, one way or another, she was going to make sure he was going to benefit from Harry's generosity. Not that she wouldn't have been grateful for it, had the circumstances been different

— had the money rightfully been Harry's to hand over.

'You spend a penny of that money on me and there will be trouble.' The smile reached his eyes and Rosie found herself smiling back. 'Seriously, that money was paid over in exchange for the manor — the fact my brother paid over the odds isn't your problem. Okay?'

Reluctantly she nodded.

'Good. Now, maybe we should give Evie a shout,' he said.

'The car's waiting downstairs.'

Rosie frowned. She hadn't seen her sister for a while. 'Where is she anyway?'

'In the study, updating her Facebook status.'

Rosie gave a short laugh. 'And probably chatting to Louise. Honestly.'

She went through to Theo's study to tell Evie they'd be leaving soon, and then went back to Theo who had papers from his briefcase scattered all over the living room.

242

'Aren't you coming with us? It'd be nice to go sightseeing.' She bit her lip as she realised how touristy she must have sounded. 'Of course — you'll have seen everything already.'

He looked up. 'I'd like to take you sightseeing, but not today. The car's at your disposal — you can go wherever you want.'

'Oh.' She was too late to stop the exclamation of disappointment.

'Don't be like that. I really have to get some work done. We can meet up for dinner later.'

'I really don't know why you invited us up here if you're too busy to spend time with us.'

'I thought you'd enjoy the break. Besides . . . ' He hesitated and looked almost shy.

'Besides what?' she demanded.

'Well, I just wanted to see you. I've missed you.'

Instantly, all was forgiven and Rosie found herself smiling.

'I've missed you, too.' It was amazing

how much courage it took to admit that out loud.

He smiled back. 'I should be finished here by six. If you don't fancy sightseeing, take that company credit card I gave you and go mad. Treat yourself and your sister.'

'That could be a dangerous offer. How do you know Evie won't bankrupt you?'

He smiled and picked up a folder from the coffee table. 'If you come close to denting my fortune I'll warn you.'

'Meaning you're so incredibly rich I couldn't possibly do much damage to your millions.'

'Remind me to show you my bank statements sometime.' His smile widened to an out-and-out grin. 'But if the thought of shopping offends you, why don't you treat yourself to a visit to the spa and beauty parlour downstairs?'

Affronted by this suggestion, Rosie glared at him. 'I'm not some dolly bird who's happy to spend her time and your money pampering and preening herself all day. Besides, why do you think I need to visit a beauty parlour?'

'Don't pretend you even imagine I was suggesting there's anything wrong with you — you must know by now how I feel about the way you look. You're utterly beautiful.'

Rosie stared at him, stunned. And horrified and embarrassed that she'd brought this on herself. What if he thought she'd been looking for compliments? But, on the other hand, this might be as near a declaration of devotion as she'd ever get from Theo.

'I'm not beautiful.'

'You have the most amazing luminous skin, your eyes are vibrant and alive, your hair is incredible . . . '

A slow blush heated her skin. 'I'm not used to being spoken to like this.' She wasn't enjoying it, she felt horribly uncomfortable. 'Don't.'

He sighed. 'I just thought a visit to the beauty parlour would help you to relax. You've been through so much — not just since Harry sold the manor, but your whole life has been a struggle. You deserve to be pampered.'

No way did she want to be cosseted. But she supposed Theo made some kind of sense. These days she didn't even manage to visit a hairdresser. It hadn't particularly bothered her as she had been blessed with hair so curly it covered a multitude of self-inflicted sins. But, despite her usual lack of vanity, she had a sudden urge to experience life as lived by the other half.

'I could do with a haircut,' she commented absently. 'It's years since I had it cut properly.'

Theo got to his feet and advanced, his liquid gold eyes fixed on her wild red curls.

'You can have an inch cut off the length,' he warned, winding his long, dark fingers into the soft tresses. 'And no more.'

'I quite fancy having it short for a change,' she challenged, hardly able to breathe as she looked up and his free hand snaked around her waist to draw her closer.

'Don't you dare.' His lips were mere inches away from hers.

'You can't tell me how to wear my hair.'

'I'm not telling, I'm asking.' He gently kissed the top of her head. 'Nicely.'

'And what if I have it cut off anyway?'

His golden eyes met the challenge in her green ones. His lips moved closer to hers, hovered invitingly only millimetres away.

She tasted the tingle of anticipation on her lips and she hated herself for it.

'You won't,' he intoned with breathless arrogance that infuriated her to the point where she resolved to have it cut so short she'd never need to use a de-tangling comb again. And she'd probably look like a boy.

'And are these perks available to all your staff?'

'Only the ones who can make my heart beat a little faster with just a smile.'

She was aware of Evie entering the room, but resisted the urge to move away from Theo.

'I'm ready to go,' Evie announced.

'Okay,' she said, not taking her eyes from Theo, silently warning him she'd wear her hair any way she liked.

She and Evie went to the hotel's beauty parlour as Theo had suggested, but Rosie paid for their treatments herself. Much as she liked and respected Theo, taking advantage of his generous nature wasn't on her agenda. Particularly not when she was about to give orders that her unruly mop was to be shorn.

Despite her resolve, however, she found she couldn't do it. As she sat in the chair, the hairdresser at her side waiting patiently for instruction, she just couldn't bring herself to tell him to cut it all off. It wasn't vanity on her part, but the memory of the look on Theo's face as he'd spoken of how much he liked her hair long.

Although it shouldn't have mattered

to her, she found she didn't want to disappoint him. Which made no sense whatsoever. Maybe she'd grown to like Theo even more than she'd thought.

★ ★ ★

She had been looking forward to Theo travelling back to the estate with them. Even though the plan was for him to spend a week or so reviewing the plans for the manor and estate, she'd also relished the prospect of spending time with him. But, in the end, work kept him in London.

'I'll do my best to come down tomorrow,' he promised as Rosie and Evie got into the car for the drive home.

Rosie couldn't quash her feelings of disappointment. Which was daft because she'd always known, with Theo, his high-flying wheeling and dealing would come first. And why wouldn't it? There was no reason why he should put her before the commitment he'd made to his company.

She moved the estate office to Farnham House the next day. It made sense, primarily because it was impossible to work at the manor with an army of workmen knocking seven bells out of the place. In addition, Rosie didn't want to be around to see her old home being pulled apart. It was bad enough to have all the strangers bustling about when they were just at the planning and prepping stage — but a complete remodelling was planned. The manor would never be the same again.

Away from the noise and dust, she got a surprising amount of work done. Glancing at the clock, she frowned; nearly seven o'clock already. Where had the day gone?

She was about to go and look for something to eat when the telephone rang. With a sigh, she answered.

'Hello?' Needing to move from her desk, she wandered out to the hall with the cordless receiver balanced between ear and shoulder.

'Rosie, it's me.' Theo's voice reverberated, making her shiver. She sank onto the stairs before her knees gave way.

'Hi.' Why was it she couldn't help smiling when she heard his voice?

'What are you doing?'

She sighed. 'I was just about to finish off for the day.'

'You're still working?'

'I am. But if you're going to tell me off you're on pretty shaky ground — as you're still not here, I'm guessing you're still working too. And that you won't be arriving as planned today.'

He sighed softly. 'You don't mind?'

'I'm not in any position to mind.'

'I'll see you as soon as I can.'

'I'm sure you will.' She tried hard to keep her tone bright, she didn't want him to know how much she'd been looking forward to seeing him.

'Is Evie home?'

'No. I haven't seen her since this morning. She went to the sanctuary straight from school and then home with Louise for tea and a study session.'

'I don't like to think of you alone.'

'I'm a big girl, I'm fine. Besides, she'll be home soon.'

'I'll call you later,' he promised. 'To say goodnight.'

She found she quite liked that idea.

Moments later, she heard a car drive up on the gravel outside. At first she thought perhaps Theo had been teasing her by ringing from the car, and he'd come back tonight after all. But then she heard two doors slamming and happy voices as Evie and Julia made their way indoors. Heads together, they were giggling and chatting. Watching them come inside, Rosie felt strangely detached. They stopped, noticing her on the stairs.

'Hi, you two.' She didn't get up — the stairs were surprisingly comfy as an impromptu seat.

'Gosh — wasn't expecting to see you sitting there, you gave me quite a fright. Is everything okay?' Julia's greeting was overly bright — almost forced.

Rosie was puzzled. 'I'm fine. Are you okay?'

'Rosie — we have something to tell you,' Evie broke in.

Rosie smiled at Evie's enthusiasm. And was further worried by Julia's sharp intake of breath. Something wasn't right.

'What is it? Good news, I hope?'

Evie grinned. 'Wonderful news.'

'Well, tell me. I could use some wonderful news.'

Rosie didn't want to admit it, but Theo not turning up tonight had upset her. Maybe that's why she'd picked up on a vibe something wasn't right with Julia — transference of anxiety.

Evie glanced questioningly at Julia as the older woman sat down next to Rosie on the stairs and dropped an arm casually around her shoulder.

'Where's the boss?' she asked. 'I thought he was going to be here tonight.'

'He had to stay in London. He'll be down as soon as he can.' She looked from Julia to Evie. 'What's this hot news item?'

'Thing is ... ' Evie was grinning from ear to ear. 'Julia's my aunt! She wants me to go and live with her and Bob and Louise. We're going to be a family. Isn't that great?'

A hint of a smile still played around Rosie's lips. She shook her head, unable to comprehend. Evie wasn't making any sense.

'You don't have an aunt. Dad was an only child, remember.'

'No,' Evie explained with infinite patience. 'Julia's my mother's sister.'

'Your mother is a woman named Glory,' Rosie explained just as patiently, as she had a thousand times. 'She left shortly after you were born. We don't know what happened to her. And, as far as we know, she didn't have any family.'

Julia sent Evie a silencing look. 'I really didn't want to tell you this while you're on your own. This is going to be rough — I'd hoped Theo would be here to take care of you.'

'What are you talking about? I don't need anyone to take care of me. What's going to be rough?' Rosie demanded.

'I'd rather wait until Theo gets back . . . '

'You can't start a conversation like this and leave it hanging. I need to know now. Why does Evie think you're her aunt? What happened to Glory?'

Julia sighed. 'All right. Glory's dead.'

'Dead?' Rosie's lips were numb, the word barely more than a whisper. 'How?'

'Pneumonia. She was never strong, not even as a child. But, emotionally, she found it hard to cope with not being allowed to see Evie. It took its toll on her. She was in and out of hospital with various ailments over those past few years.'

This didn't make sense. 'She left Evie. It was her decision.'

'My sister Gloria — Glory, as you knew her — was seriously off the rails when she got involved with your father. She was only twenty, but moved in with and then married a rock star who was decades older. Doesn't that speak volumes to you about her state of mind?'

'But why would she lie? Why would she say she wasn't allowed to see Evie?'

'Your father warned Glory to stay away — told her she was an unfit mother, that he'd fight for custody. Against him she didn't think she stood a chance.'

Rosie racked her brains for some long-buried memories.

'But it doesn't make sense.'

Julia tucked her hair behind her ear. Rosie had noticed before that she did that a lot — especially when she was stressed.

'In the end, Glory guessed she didn't have long left. She begged me to promise that, if she died, I'd look out for Evie. She knew I couldn't have children of my own and that I'd be more than happy to do it. But your father wouldn't let me near.'

'That still doesn't explain why you

didn't admit who you were when you moved to the village.'

'When I heard your father had died, I thought that was my chance to get my sister's little girl back. But I didn't want to be too heavy-handed about it because I didn't want to upset Evie — and she would have been upset if some stranger had taken her away. So I moved to the area, met and married Bob. But by then I'd became friends with you and saw how close you and Evie were. I grew to love you both and realised I couldn't take Evie away when your life was falling apart. She was all you had.'

'But it's okay to take her away from me now?'

'Things are looking up for you now. Theo seems to have taken you under his wing and he can offer you all sorts of opportunities. You'll thrive under his mentorship — I know you will — but you will need to concentrate and work hard. That will be easier for you to do if you don't have to worry about Evie.'

Rosie glanced at her little sister, who was visibly distressed.

'I'll always worry about Evie, whoever she lives with. Besides, she's never been a burden. Theo knows she's my priority.'

'Nobody would ever accuse you of not putting Evie first, but it's time to prioritise yourself for a change. Evie wouldn't come and live with me before because she didn't want to leave you on your own, but now you have Theo . . . '

'So you *did* ask her to leave me? Despite what you said earlier.' Rosie shrugged Julia's arm from her shoulder.

'Not exactly . . . but the time came when I felt it was right to tell her. Obviously we discussed what should happen.'

'But you didn't think to include me in your discussions?'

Julia looked uncomfortable. 'We didn't want to upset you.'

Evie had known. Julia and Glory were sisters and Evie had known and not said anything. Rosie turned her attention to Evie. 'How long ago did she tell you?'

Evie stared guiltily at the floor. 'A while.'

'Why didn't you say?'

'No point. I was never going to leave you on your own. You always said we were a team; that was how I saw it too.'

'But you don't think we're a team any longer?'

Evie looked uncomfortable. 'It's just now you have Theo, I thought I could maybe spend some time with Julia.'

'I don't 'have' Theo. He's my boss — that's all.'

'He wants to be more,' Julia added gently. 'And if you have time to sort yourself out, I think you'll find you want that, too.'

Rosie was stunned. The two people she thought were closest to her in the world and they didn't know her at all.

'You should have told me the truth as soon as you found out, Evie.' She bit her lip. 'You could have told me and not moved in with her — didn't that occur to you?'

'Rosie, please.' Evie shook her head. 'I just didn't want to hurt you. And I knew if I told you Julia was really my aunt and she wanted me to live with her, it would make things awkward.'

Rosie gasped, mortified. The little sister she had loved and tried to protect had ended up trying to protect her. Suddenly it made sense that Evie had stopped talking about Glory, had stopped asking questions. Evie had known more about the situation than Rosie. And, of course, this explained why Evie had been so relaxed about leaving the manor. As long as she was close enough to her donkeys, she didn't care where she lived.

Now Rosie looked at Julia, truly looked at her, there were plenty of similarities between her and Glory. They had the same eyes, the same mannerisms — Glory had been forever tucking her hair behind her ear in the same way Julia did. How could she have failed to notice before?

'You could have told me, Evie. You know you can always tell me anything.'

Evie sniffed. 'I'm sorry.'

Rosie immediately relented. Evie feeling bad about things wouldn't accomplish anything. She held out her arms and Evie went to her, returning her hug.

'You understand?'

'I think so.'

Although it seemed her life was crashing down around her.

16

Sitting in his office at his company's headquarters, Theo couldn't shake the feeling something was wrong. He'd been trying to get through to Rosie for the past hour and there was no reply. He glanced at his watch — it was late and she hadn't mentioned earlier she'd be going out. As far as he knew, she should be home.

He hadn't been able to get Rosie out of his mind since she'd left him yesterday. The nagging urge to speak to her had been there all day. He'd kept it brief earlier, but that tiny taste had only strengthened his need to speak to her. And now he'd given into temptation to ring again and she wasn't picking up, the urge was becoming unbearable.

He tried her mobile number. Still no answer.

'Boss, I need you to look over these.'

Andy broke into his thoughts, effectively pulling his attention to a sheaf of papers needing urgent attention. He'd try to call Rosie again in a few minutes when he'd dealt with these problems.

When Andy left the room half an hour later, Theo asked him to close the door behind him. And then he tried to phone both Farnham House and Rosie's mobile again. Still no answer. Seriously worried now, he headed for the door.

'See you tomorrow, boss,' Andy called cheerfully as Theo strode through the outer office.

'I wouldn't count on it, Andy. And you need to go home, too. It's late.' He lifted his hand in farewell as he hurried to the lift.

Damn, he should have arranged for the helicopter. Too late to worry about that now; by the time he'd summoned the pilot and they were ready to take off it would be faster to drive.

All the way home, however many times he told himself he was being daft, he couldn't shake the feeling of doom. And he cursed himself for not going back with Rosie and Evie last night.

No lights burned in the windows of Farnham House as he drew up. He'd been right; something was horribly wrong.

Theo had never been a coward, but his stomach churned and his pulse raced as he prepared to get out of his car and go inside. This was fear on a massive scale.

His feet crunched ominously on the gravel as he made his way to the front door. Throwing it open, he hurried inside and turned on the hall light.

Relief flooded through him at the sight of Rosie's tiny frame huddled on the stairs. Relief turned to concern when he realised her skin held a deathly pallor and her eyes were reddened from crying. This was something much more serious than the result of him changing his plans.

'Rosie?'

She looked up at the sound of his

voice, her entire body shuddered with renewed sobs and she held out her arms to him. He covered the distance between them in a few quick strides and lifted her, holding her tight against him, letting her cry as though her heart had broken.

Slowly, cradled in Theo's arms, Rosie began to calm down. He had taken her seat on the stairs and arranged her on his lap. She was frozen through, and the hoped the closeness of his body would warm her.

After a while, she began to reveal the full horror of what had happened.

'She's really gone. I still can't believe it. After all the years I've spent raising her, it feels as though Julia's taken my child.'

Theo hated to see her in such despair.

'Why has Julia decided to speak up now? Are you sure she's telling the truth?'

'I wasn't at first,' Rosie admitted. 'I couldn't believe it. But as Julia explained, it all clicked into place. She really is Glory's sister. I could see the family resemblance. Besides, what possible reason could she have to lie about a thing like that?'

'We can fight for custody. We can get Evie back.'

She was incredibly touched that he was prepared to do that for her. For a moment, the temptation to ask him to set the lawyers on Julia hovered. But she had to think of the best thing for Evie.

'Evie deserves to spend time with her aunt — and she's the important one in all this.'

He shook his head. 'This doesn't add up. Why didn't Julia tell you? Why didn't she take Evie straight away? She moved to the village years ago. She's seen how you've struggled to keep things together. She could have made life easier for you.'

'I think she tried, but Evie wouldn't leave me. She was heartbreakingly loyal, even when offered the chance of an easier life with her aunt and best friend's family. I've got to let her have this, however much it hurts me.'

'But why did she speak up now, after all this time?'

Rosie's eyes were clear and green.

'Because she thinks I've got you.'

Theo was gutted. In trying to give Rosie what she wanted — a job and a secure home for her younger sister — he'd been responsible for her worst nightmare. Because of him, her sister had gone.

As soon as Rosie came to her senses and realised the truth, she'd blame him. Even worse, she would hate him. And he would have no means of holding on to her. The estate would mean nothing to her without Evie.

'I don't understand why I didn't recognise Julia from the beginning. I should have known. She's not unlike Glory.'

'You weren't expecting her to deceive you. You took her friendship at face value.'

'And it blew up in my face,' she retorted bitterly. 'I'm beginning to think I can't trust anyone.'

'You can trust me.' He hated himself for the lie. Even while he offered comfort, he was plotting ways to keep her with him.

She leaned into his shoulder. 'I know I can.'

Something twisted in Theo's gut.

He carried her to the sitting room, where she eventually fell into an exhausted sleep on the sofa. He turned out the lamps, covered her with a duvet he found upstairs and settled on a nearby chair to watch her sleep by the muted light escaping from the hall. She shouldn't be left alone when she was so upset.

*　*　*

Eventually, she stirred.

'Theo?' Her voice came in a frantic whisper.

'It's okay, I'm here.'

'I dreamed it never happened and she was still here.'

'She hasn't gone far. You'll still see her. Try to sleep.'

She shook her head. 'Not yet. Talk to me.'

'What about?'

'Your family — your parents. What were they like?'

Not really where he wanted to go. Theo sighed, and hoped the lighting was dim enough to hide the reluctance undoubtedly etched on his face.

'My parents certainly married for love, but the example they presented wasn't exactly a glowing advertisement for wedded bliss.' He sighed.

'But they did love each other?'

'So they insisted, but there was little evidence. They met when my father was on holiday in Greece — Mum left her family to be with him. They never forgave her. It might not have been so bad if they'd been happy, but they weren't.'

Rosie was horrified. 'And you saw that?'

He shrugged. 'We got over it. Mum died when Lysander and I were both quite young and things calmed down a bit after that.'

'What did she die of?'

'A previously undiagnosed heart defect.'

'How old were you then, Theo?' she asked him softly.

'Eleven.'

That was another thing they had in common, he reflected — dysfunctional parents, unhappy childhoods, the loss of their mother at a young age.

'What about Gina?' she asked sleepily.

'What about her?'

'Did you love her?'

'No.' He answered instantly. No doubt at all about that. 'I've never been in love.'

Rosie relaxed against the cushions once again. As she drifted back to sleep, what had remained unsaid played on his mind. Those early views of love and relationships had been further compounded by the empty relationships

Theo had himself endured as an adult. He'd been wary of committing himself from the outset, preferring to concentrate on business interests, but a certain type of woman had battled relentlessly past his outward defences.

Unfortunately, those women had been vain and mercenary and had thought nothing of simpering vacuous and meaningless words of love. But their idea of love had been measured in terms of his bank balance and his willingness to pick up the bills for shoes and handbags.

That's why he was fascinated by Rosie. Lovely Rosie, who didn't want anything for herself and who argued whenever he tried to spoil her. Even if he didn't love her, he'd be a fool to let her get away.

And, if he ever changed his mind, he imagined it would be very easy to fall in love with Rosie.

★ ★ ★

Rosie woke up and Theo was gone. As she registered that fact, the memory of yesterday rushed into her head. She was surprised she'd managed to sleep at all. Already the ache of missing Evie presented as a sharp pain in her chest. It was one thing for Evie to stay as a guest with Julia and her family; quite another for her to move out to live with them permanently.

And Rosie was so furious with Julia, it wasn't true. She'd lied. Wormed her way into Rosie's confidence — pretended to be her best friend.

'How are you this morning?' Theo brought in a mug of tea and put it down on the side table.

'Thanks.' Rosie elbowed her way out of the duvet, picked up the mug and sipped. 'I needed that. I've been better. I still feel all kinds of stupid for not realising there was something not quite right about the Julia situation.'

'Don't be so hard on yourself.' The cushions shifted as he sat easily at her feet. He looked as though he belonged there. 'You took her friendship at face value.'

'I should have known — she was always so keen to help. So eager to have Evie stay over. It wasn't normal.'

'Evie and Julia's stepdaughter are friends. They've worked together, running the sanctuary, and they help each other with homework. Why would you suspect anything else was going on?'

'I suppose.' She took another sip of her tea, then glanced at Theo from beneath her lashes. 'I thought you'd gone.'

He smiled and reached out to rest his hand on her ankle. Through the cover, she could feel the weight of his touch and was comforted by it. More comforted than she should have been. She liked having him around. Liked having him to rely on.

'I didn't want to leave you.'

Physical pain squeezed her heart at his admission and that was the exact moment the truth hit her with all the subtlety of a jackhammer — she was desperately in love with Theo Bradley.

It had been building up gradually and now, at the most inconvenient time possible, it threatened to overwhelm her.

She took a deep breath. She had to leave the estate, there was no other choice under the circumstances. Evie was no longer a consideration. And Theo didn't want love. If he ever found out how she felt about him, she'd be on the next bus out of his life — probably on the seat next to Gina.

'I would have been fine.'

He smiled again, and it was as though his gold glance was a whisper against her skin.

'I preferred to stay and see for myself.'

She didn't want to move. Once she was up, she'd have to face the reality of life without Evie — and the reality of loving Theo. While she stayed wrapped in her duvet, she didn't have to think. But she was still dressed in yesterday's clothes, her head heavy from hours of crying.

'I need a shower.'

'I'll have breakfast ready when you're dressed.'

Was there no end to the man's talents? Really, he was just about perfect, she realised as she turned the shower full on and stepped under. Too perfect for her.

Theo must never find out she was in love with him. Their relationship was a business one bordering on friendship, nothing more, and she had to remember that. It was not appropriate for her to allow her feelings to become involved. Besides which, this was her worst nightmare come true. She'd spent her life believing that falling in love would make her no better than her father's groupies, and now she was in danger of behaving exactly like them.

But how in heaven's name was she supposed to hide the fact she loved him? And, more to the point, how could she quash those feelings when he insisted on being lovely at every turn? It frightened the life out of her.

By falling for Theo so completely, she had laid herself wide open for betrayal in the most devastating way. Everyone she had ever been close to had done their bit to mess her life up — her father, her brother, even Julia. It looked as though betrayal went with the territory when you cared for someone.

And she cared for Theo more than she'd ever cared for anyone. Theo had the ability to hurt her more than any other human being ever had. She didn't want him to have that power.

She didn't want to be in love with him.

Fear gripped her. What she felt for Theo was so much more than she had expected love to be. He'd become the entire focus of her life, surpassing even her grief that Evie had gone. She waited around for any crumb of attention he deigned to drop her way. Just as her father's girlfriends had hung around him waiting for his attention to validate their own existences.

He was busy at the Aga when she

reached the kitchen.

'Bacon and eggs okay for you?' he asked cheerfully.

'Mmm, lovely, thank you.'

She grabbed a piece of toast and began to chew mechanically. She was going to have to be so careful. She couldn't afford for him to guess — or she and Evie would be evicted before they knew it.

And then she remembered she was leaving and that Evie had another home now. And the sense of loss started to bite at her anew.

Theo could see the shutters closing over her lovely green eyes. This morning she'd turned back into a stranger — completely closed off — and it was obvious she didn't want to share any of the thoughts going through her beautiful head. He'd noticed that she still wore her old jeans in preference to anything in the smart new wardrobe he had provided her with. He'd been so sure they'd reached an understanding recently, but it seemed they were back to square one.

Today wasn't a day to ask about those things, though. Regardless of her reluctance to share, he knew she must be hurting badly. Today she needed to be looked after, cosseted and reassured.

'She hasn't gone far.' He flipped the bacon and cast a sympathetic glance in her direction.

'I know. I'm glad for her. Really I am. She's getting the chance to make a life away from the estate — and from the shadow of our father's behaviour.'

That was more than Rosie ever had, he realised grimly. She had sacrificed any chance of a life of her own to raise her sister. The more he found out about Rosie, the more he admired her.

'Evie will be back to visit.'

He glanced at her, uneasy he'd exploited her need to provide a home for her sister and her attachment to the estate for his own ends. He'd been too eager to take her up on her offer to run the place — despite knowing it probably wasn't in her best interest —

because he'd wanted to keep her close. He realised that now. And he could admit to himself that the attraction between them had floored him from the beginning.

'Well, she'll be back to see the donkeys.'

He smiled as she made a brave attempt at humour. He blamed himself entirely for this. He'd messed up big time. In trying to give her what she wanted, he'd facilitated this disaster — breaking Rosie's heart in the process.

'She'll be back to see you. You're still her sister and she still loves you.'

Rosie nodded, but it was obvious she was fighting back tears.

'Thank you for staying with me last night. I don't know how I would have managed on my own.'

'That's what I'm here for.'

'But you were supposed to be at work. In fact, shouldn't you be there now?'

Yes, he should be — this diversion had the potential to lose him millions.

But Rosie was more important.

'They'll cope without me.' He served up the food and brought the plates over to where she sat at the table. 'I thought, perhaps, under the circumstances, you might like to come back to London with me for a few days.'

That got her attention. Her head snapped up and she stared at him across the table. 'What?' Her eyes narrowed. 'Why?'

He shrugged. 'Why not? Maybe we could go on that sightseeing trip you suggested. Besides, if you're here on your own I'll worry about you.' He hardly dared to breathe as he waited for her answer.

'I can't think about this now, Theo.'

'You need a few days away from the estate.'

Her eyes widened and he couldn't help noticing she didn't look happy at the prospect. 'I can't leave the estate now — not with the renovations about to start on the manor.'

'There's a management team on

standby, ready to step in and hold the fort for you.'

'And I don't want to be too far away in case Evie needs me.'

He sat back and folded his arms as he regarded her thoughtfully. She was making excuses now. He knew better than to push, but still he couldn't help himself.

'If she does, she can phone. You can come straight back to her,' he reasoned.

She shook her head, her eyes dull, her lovely mouth downturned. It seemed as though the ground was falling away beneath his chair.

'You're right, Theo. There's no reason for me to stay. And as you already have a team on standby, I'd like to hand in my notice. I'll be leaving the estate as soon as I can tie up all the loose ends.'

He knew then that he'd lost her.

17

Rosie was torn as she watched Theo leave. She wanted to call out after him, to stop him. He'd looked as devastated as she felt, but she knew there was no way she could stay. Not when she was so in love with him.

Best to end it now, before he discovered her sad little secret. She was sure he would be kind — he would pity her for her foolish lack of self-restraint. He would feel sorry for her because she was every bit as weak as her father and his army of female followers. And then she would have to endure his sympathy as he told her he didn't return her feelings.

She knew that would kill her.

When she heard the front door crash open, she thought he'd come back and her heart leapt. She tried not to show her fleeting disappointment when Evie rushed in. And then she realised Evie had been crying, and thoughts of Theo were pushed to the back of her mind.

'Evie, what's wrong?'

'George,' she cried on the peak of a sob. 'He said I care more about Jessie than I do about him!'

A lover's tiff. Rosie heaved a sigh of relief. It wasn't the end of the world, even though it might feel like it to Evie at the moment. 'What did you say to that?'

'I told him it was true.' She wailed again. 'But it's so not.'

'Oh sweetheart, come here.'

Evie obliged and, still sobbing, walked towards Rosie's outstretched arms. Rosie was tempted to join in as Evie cried against her shoulder, but she had to be strong — if she gave into temptation, she'd cry for the rest of her life.

'It will be okay, I promise.' She stroked Evie's hair and made more soothing noises. 'What did Julia say?'

'She thinks it's for the best — that he's too old for me.'

Rosie thought back to the conversation she'd had with Julia just after discovering Evie was serious about George. She'd thought it odd at the time that Julia had been so adamant Rosie needed to put a stop to it, but now she knew why. She hadn't been speaking as an interested friend, but as a concerned aunt.

'She's only worried about you. And three years, at your age, is quite a gap.'

'But I love him.'

Rosie's heart lurched. Evie had grown up so quickly. It seemed only yesterday that she was playing with dolls and now she had a boyfriend, plans for university and a future.

'I know you do. And I think he loves you.'

As she spoke, the doorbell rang. 'That could well be him now. You put the kettle on and I'll go and see.'

But it wasn't George. It was Julia. She gave a half-smile.

'I didn't know if I'd be welcome.'

'I'm hardly going to ban you from

the house.' Rosie stood aside awkwardly to let her in. 'Evie's here. She's upset.'

Julia nodded as she stepped past. 'George is looking for her. He's gone to the sanctuary, but I thought she might be here.'

Rosie lifted an eyebrow.

'Well, who else is she going to run to when she's upset?'

There was a flurry as Evie rushed into the hall; it was obvious she'd heard. 'George is looking for me at the sanctuary?' Evie ran towards the front door, pulling her coat back on as she went. 'Gotta-go. Thanks, Rosie.'

She stopped long enough to peck Rosie on the cheek and to smile through her tears at Julia, and then she was gone.

Rosie and Julia looked at each other for a long moment and then simultaneously burst out laughing. 'Another drama over,' Julia said.

Although Rosie understood Evie had been broken-hearted, it was still amusing to see how quickly her sister had recovered her usual bounce once she heard George wanted to make up.

'What did they argue about?'

'Something and nothing. Evie wanted him to help with the donkeys because some of her volunteers had called in sick, but he wanted to practise his music. She took it seriously at the time, though.'

Rosie nodded and shifted uncomfortably. This was awkward. But she could hardly ignore Julia, not when she'd been a friend for so many years. And particularly not now it was known she was Evie's aunt.

'Do you have time for a coffee?'

It would take her time to forgive the deception, but maybe, given time, they might be able to rebuild their friendship.

Julia gave a relieved sigh. 'Actually, I'd love a coffee.'

Once seated at the kitchen table with their drinks Julia spoke.

'I'm so sorry. I should have owned up years ago, but I didn't know how to tell you. I really wanted to get to know Evie first. And the more I got to know you both, the harder I found it to own up. You were in a pretty vulnerable position when I first turned up — you'd just lost your father and found he'd left you nothing. I thought if I took Evie away it would just make matters worse. And I didn't want that. I care about you, too.'

'I think if you'd taken Evie to live with you at that point, I'd have lost it completely,' Rosie admitted. 'And I do appreciate everything you've done for us since you moved to the area. I would never have managed without your help. But I can't help feeling foolish that I didn't realise.'

'How could you have known?'

'The clues were there — the way you were always too eager to have Evie in your home. You even took her on holiday with you and Bob and Louise.'

Julia shrugged. 'That was nothing, I wanted to do so much more. But you wouldn't take any financial help, and until I told you the truth I couldn't insist.'

Rosie took a long gulp of her drink and winced as the hot liquid burned her tongue. 'Did Glory tell you why she left?'

'She and your dad weren't getting along. She was very young, much younger than him. He made it clear Evie would be better off if she went. She watched from a distance, but she didn't dare come back — even though she hated being apart from her only child.'

'I'm sorry. It can't have been easy, seeing your little sister die.' Rosie thought for a moment how she'd feel in the same situation and recoiled from the image.

'It was hard,' Julia admitted. 'I still miss her.'

That was one of the reasons Evie was so important to Julia. Rosie understood now. She also understood what it must have cost Julia to stand by and say nothing all these years. If she hadn't been such a good friend, she could have claimed Evie years ago.

'Any word from Theo?' Julia obviously wanted to change the subject and Rosie was inclined to let her — even though her choice of diversion wasn't the best.

'He came down late last night. But he's gone now. I handed in my notice. Doubt I'll see him again.'

'What? But he won't let you go, surely.'

'He already has done. It's time I made my own way in the world, anyway.' She made a brave attempt at a smile.

'He'll be back.'

Rosie wasn't happy Julia was pressing the issue. 'I don't think he will.'

Julie laughed. 'If he's not a man in love I'll eat my hat.'

'He doesn't love me. And he doesn't want me to love him.'

'But you do.'

Rosie couldn't bring herself to deny it. 'Is it so obvious?'

'Only to those who care about you.'

By extrapolation of that statement, Theo obviously didn't care about her, but Rosie didn't want to dwell on it.

'I'm so worried I'm turning into one of those women — the ones who flocked to the estate when I was growing up. They were all so needy. They threw themselves at my father and he was so shallow and treated them dreadfully.'

'Well, you're nobody's doormat,' Julia assured her friend without a moment's hesitation. 'In fact you're the very opposite of those women. They couldn't have loved your father — they would have barely known him. They threw themselves at a stranger. But you've waited for the real thing with Theo.'

She gave a small shrug. 'But it's not what he wants.'

Things were easier between them after that. Rosie could see a way forward where she and Julia could still be friends — and not just for Evie's sake. Deception aside, Julia had done all she could for both Evie and Rosie over the past five years. She had been a good friend and it had obviously been a genuine friendship, not a façade for Evie's benefit.

*   *   *

Rosie made a concerted effort to get on with her work once Julia had left. She'd lost so much time already today with all the interruptions. Not to mention her heartbreak when the love of her life had left. Work always gave her a focus, provided a diversion, and she'd never needed one more. Besides, it was important she leave everything in order — to make the handover to Theo's new team as seamless as possible.

She didn't hear anyone come into the house, but something made her look up and they were there, in the doorway of her office. Lysander — and some weedy-looking sidekick.

'It's customary to knock before

barging into someone's home.' She knew she was being rude, but she really wasn't in the mood to be pleasant.

'My brother happens to own this house and everything else on this estate. I'm sure he won't mind.' He sneered at her and she wanted to slap him.

'Didn't he tell you to keep away from us?'

She hadn't taken to Lysander during their brief meeting at Chudley House, and his behaviour now did nothing to change her original opinion. He made her feel uncomfortable in the extreme. He sauntered into the room without invitation.

'Theo isn't here.' She remained seated, using her desk as a safety barrier between herself and the intruders.

'Of course he's not here, he'll be at work. Where else would a workaholic be?'

She was tempted to offer a caustic retort of the order that she was surprised he'd know how a workaholic operated, but she decided against it. She didn't want an argument. She just wanted Lysander to leave, as soon as humanly possible.

'Can I give him a message?'

'No message. It's you I came to see.' He glanced over his shoulder at his companion. 'Jim, there must be a kitchen around here somewhere, go and make some tea.'

Rosie was outraged. 'Hey. Don't go telling strangers to waltz off around my home helping themselves to beverages. And what do you what to see me for, anyway?'

'I was talking to Harry — he said he was worried about you. He seems to think you have designs on Theo — and that you're after him for his money.'

'Never!' Rosie flushed an angry pink. It had absolutely not been about the money. She'd convinced herself at first it had been about friendship, but even when she'd denied to herself she was in love with him, she'd never been tempted to even imagine that her interest in him had been to do with his money.

'No need to play the innocent around me — I know exactly what you're like. You used your sister to bleed Harry dry for years. He was desperate when I met him — utterly desperate. That's why I put him out of his misery and paid far too much for your rundown dump of an estate. You're nothing but a gold-digger, and you must have thought all your Christmases had arrived at once when poor Theo landed on your doorstep.'

'Harry was desperate because he'd been gambling and lost — nothing to do with me or Evie. Besides, Evie was just as much his responsibility as mine.'

Lysander paced the floor, picked up a paperweight from Rosie's desk and transferred it from one hand to the other. She wished he wouldn't, it was very annoying.

'Perhaps that's true.' His grin made her cringe. 'Regardless, it seems you're now intent on convincing poor Theo to provide for you for life.'

Rosie was outraged. 'Not that it's any of your business, but I work. I have a proper salaried position. Besides, if it's true Harry's so worried, why didn't he come to see me himself?'

Lysander shrugged dismissively. 'Oh, come, surely you know Harry by now — emotional scenes just aren't his thing.'

Rosie shook her head. 'I don't believe for a second that Harry sent you.' She knew they had some way to go, but her brother had seemed so keen to make amends. And she wanted her relationship with him to work far too much to sit listening to Lysander spouting poison. 'I don't have time for this, I have work to do,' she informed the intruder.

'You don't have to pretend. I know Theo will have set you up very nicely. I'm a bit upset about it all, actually. I could do with you disappearing from the scene.'

'What's it got to do with you?'

'Well, you've just met my friend, Jim. He has a property development company and he could cram a lot of little houses onto this estate.'

'What would be in it for you?'

'Money, of course. If I could pull off a deal like that, Theo would have to give me a cut of the profits. Leave the estate, Rosie, before I have to do something you'll regret.'

It would be so easy to tell him she'd already made the decision to go, but she had no intention of giving in to a bully-boy like him.

'I don't respond to threats. Besides, even if I were to leave, Theo would never sell the estate. He's made promises to the people who live and work here.'

'The thing is, I'm not the only one upset about your plans to trap Theo. Gina's back in the country and distraught that Theo seems to be falling for you. She's telling everyone she'll have him back within the month.'

'Theo's told me all about Gina. I

don't feel threatened in the slightest by her.'

'You should. Gina's stunning.'

'And yet Theo still spends his free time here, with me.' Why was she arguing? She had no rights over Theo. If Gina wanted him, he was free to rekindle their relationship.

'She's nearly six feet tall, dark flowing hair, supermodel looks . . . the exact opposite of you, in fact. She has men eating out of her hand. If she's saying she wants Theo back, then I'm warning you that you should be worried.'

'You're wasting your breath, Lysander.' Rosie felt the sting of tears at the back of her eyes and was saved only by Jim returning with a tea tray.

'Be mother, Jim,' Lysander called to him as he put the tray on Rosie's desk. 'You'll take tea with us, Rosie.'

This was surreal. People didn't arrive uninvited in other people's homes to warn them to leave town by sunrise, and then make tea. Time to put a stop to this. She stood up and glared.

'Get out, Lysander — and take Jim with you. Theo will be back soon and he won't be happy to find you here.'

She wished it wasn't a lie — there was nothing she wouldn't give for Theo to walk into the house now.

'We have time for a cup of tea.' He brandished a cup and saucer in front of her. 'Have a cup of tea with us, Rosie, and then we'll go.'

She just wanted them to leave, so it seemed easier to take the cup and saucer from him and sip the hot tea than to argue.

'This tea tastes odd,' she commented.

'Jim's going to be very upset if you complain his tea doesn't taste nice.'

She took another sip. It definitely wasn't right. She put the drink down on the desk, instinct warning her that all wasn't well.

'There — I've had a drink, now please leave.' She was beginning to feel very light-headed. She just wanted to lie down.

She fell back onto her chair and

rested her head on the desk — just for a minute, she told herself.

Lysander was standing unbearably close — the cloying stench of his cologne reached her nose and made it hard to breathe.

'I don't feel well.'

'You'll be okay.' Lysander's unpleasant grin was going in and out of focus in a most alarming fashion. And he seemed to be holding a camera. 'But once my brother sees the evidence of you getting cosy with Jim — well, let's just say I won't need to ask you again to leave him alone.'

And then, with his laughter filling her ears, everything went completely black.

18

'What do you think, boss?' Andy's voice broke into Theo's thoughts and brought him back to the present. He looked around the room at the suited posse of business people awaiting his response and realised he didn't have the faintest idea what was going on. Apart from the fact this meeting wasn't going well.

His judgment was way off and it worried him that he couldn't focus with his customary singlemindedness. But what worried him even more was that he didn't care. He only cared that, when he'd left her, Rosie had been unhappy.

He hadn't gone far. He'd set up shop at Chudley House, unable to stomach the thought of being too great a distance away from her.

Rosie had come to mean more to him than just an employee — much, much more. And Theo Bradley didn't fail . . . not even at human things like relationships. It was exactly why he'd avoided them until now — and exactly why he was determined his relationship with Rosie would succeed.

But Rosie didn't want him. She no longer wanted to even work for him. And he didn't know what to do about it.

When he'd called this meeting, he'd been convinced work was the answer. He'd planned to immerse himself in this complicated business deal and allow his subconscious to work on a solution to the Rosie problem. And he'd been convinced the answer would come.

Everyone was still staring at him as though he'd gone crazy — which he supposed he had. He pushed back from his desk and got to his feet.

'I'm very much afraid, ladies and gentlemen, that I'm going to have to leave you in Andy's capable hands.'

He was aware of everyone watching

open-mouthed as he left the room.

He shouldn't have left her today. He should have stayed. Never mind work — he was the boss and he wouldn't sack himself. Besides, he'd trained Andy well and things would have progressed much better without Theo in this frame of mind, in any case.

The truth hit him with a lightning force as he made his way outside — he was in love with Rosie. Had probably loved her from the moment he had first seen her. That could be the only explanation for his absurd behaviour — for his keeping and renovating the manor in the face of all reason.

He needed to see her. Now. He knew she had no interest in a romantic relationship, but he had to try to convince her. Even if it meant making himself vulnerable by confessing his feelings.

On a whim, he dropped into the village's tiny florist on his way back to the estate and shocked himself by buying an armful of red roses. He'd never bought a woman flowers before — he'd never enjoyed that kind of relationship. His women had gratefully received jewellery and shopping trips, but he'd always thought flowers too personal.

Somehow, though, it seemed right to buy flowers for Rosie. He imagined she would appreciate them much more than she had appreciated the expensive shopping trip he'd financed. He was a man on a mission — a mission to convince Rosie to love him back. And he approached the task with the same zeal as he dealt with business challenges. Rosie would be wooed and romanced with relentless enthusiasm. And he would work until his dying day to convince her to fall in love with him.

He dropped the roses onto the passenger seat of his car and was about to set off when his mobile buzzed to life. He didn't recognise the number but answered the call, resolving to keep it brief.

'Bradley.'

'Hi there. My name's Harry Farnham. Please don't hang up.'

Not one of his favourite people, even if he'd never met the man. Theo frowned.

'What do you want, Farnham? And how did you get my number?' he barked.

'From Lysander's mobile — he's left it at home. Listen, I need you to make sure Rosie's okay.'

Theo didn't like the way this conversation was heading. An unease began to gnaw at him. 'Why wouldn't she be okay?'

'Well, thing is, Lysander wasn't very happy about you appointing Rosie to manage the estate. Seemed to think it will scupper his chances of making any money out of the place.'

Theo wanted to reach down the phone and shake Harry warmly by the throat until he said what he had to say. Instead, he gave a short, humourless laugh. 'It's not Rosie managing the estate that will do that. And if this call is an attempt to get some money, you're wasting your time.'

'It's nothing like that.' Harry's outraged tone might have been more convincing if Theo hadn't known about the years he'd spent demanding money from his sister. 'Thing is, Lysander was talking about going over to the estate. I'm worried he might hurt Rosie. He was in such a fury. I'd never forgive myself if something happened to her.'

Theo didn't wait to hear any more. He disconnected, tossed the mobile onto the seat beside the roses and roared off towards Farnham House.

He wondered if he should have called the police. But he was so close he would be there in moments and pausing, even briefly, to make a phone call hadn't seemed the best idea. Besides, he had no proof Lysander was even there. Chances were, Rosie was fine — and he kept telling himself that every moment of the way.

But, when he arrived at the house and saw Lysander's car, he knew Harry had been telling the truth. He raced in and met Lysander strolling through the hall, carrying a camera and calling for a man named Jim to meet him in the office.

'What have you done with her?' Theo's voice was low and menacing. In Lysander's place he would have answered without hesitation. 'Where's Rosie?'

'Passed out, old chap.' His brother's words were at odds with his cheerful demeanour. 'You really should be a bit more careful about the company you keep. This one's even worse than that Gina person.'

Theo had never wanted to kill anyone before, but he wanted to rip his brother's head off. His priority was to find Rosie, though, so Lysander's punishment would have to wait.

'Are you going to tell me where she is? Or do I have to beat the information out of you?'

Lysander nodded towards Rosie's office and Theo flew through the door to find her lying pale and lifeless on the floor.

She was dead!

Blood whooshed against his ear drums and a wave of nausea nearly knocked him flat. It was only his urgent need to get to Rosie's side that prevented him from passing out on the spot. He placed two fingers gently on the pulse spot on her neck and relief overwhelmed him as he felt a strong, steady heartbeat. She wasn't dead; just out cold.

'Told you — she's sozzled.'

He leapt up and rounded on Lysander, holding him by the throat against the wall. 'What have you done to her?' He didn't believe Lysander for a second. There was no way she was drunk; it would be obvious to anyone that she'd been drugged.

'Nothing.'

It would be so easy to apply a little more pressure until his brother found it impossible to draw breath. But he needed to find out what Rosie had been given. He gritted his teeth.

'Tell me now, or there will be consequences.'

Lysander must have read the murderous intent in Theo's expression, because he crumpled. 'It's nothing — a sedative, that's all. A fast-acting sedative I bought off the internet. She'll be fine once she's slept it off.'

'Why would you give her a sedative?'

Lysander shrugged against the wall and Theo tightened his hold, in a warning gesture. 'I . . . er . . . we were just having a bit of fun. We didn't mean much harm.'

'We?'

'My friend Jim and I. It was a practical Joke, nothing more.'

'Do you see anyone laughing?' Theo's fist collided painfully with Lysander's jaw — Theo only wished he'd hit him harder. But he was beneath contempt and Theo wasn't going to waste another moment — the police could deal with him later. Theo's priority was Rosie — he needed to get her to hospital, and fast.

He was aware of brushing past another man as he rushed out with Rosie in his arms, but didn't stop. Nothing mattered now but getting medical attention for Rosie. With care, he placed her in the back seat and set off. The hospital run was becoming too familiar — he hoped this would be the last time he was forced to make an emergency dash.

* * *

After the medical staff had taken blood and conducted all manner of other tests, they allowed him to sit with Rosie in her private room as she slept. She looked like a fragile doll against the starched white linen — her vibrant red hair the only colour.

It had to be the longest night of Theo's life as he attempted to contemplate life without Rosie. And he realised a life without her would be empty. He could accept she didn't love him, but he

309

knew he would be able to make her happy. And he would spend every waking moment trying to convince her of that.

Eventually, as the dawn light began to break, Rosie's eyes fluttered open. A relieved sigh escaped as she focused on him.

'Hi, Sleeping Beauty,' he murmured.

She coughed. And then croaked something.

'Have some water.' He half filled a glass and slipped his arm under her shoulders, propping her up as he held the glass to her lips and encouraged her to sip.

'Thanks.' She smiled groggily and Theo thought he'd never seen any smile as beautiful. He put the glass down and sat gingerly on the edge of the bed — close enough so that she could reach out and touch him if she wanted.

'How are you feeling?'

'Odd. Strange. What happened? Where am I?'

'Lysander gave you something — a

sedative. You're in hospital — we've been waiting for you to wake up.'

'The tea . . . ' She frowned. 'He insisted I had a cup of tea and it tasted weird. What are you doing here?'

'Harry called to warn me Lysander was planning something. When I arrived at the house, you'd passed out.'

'You brought me here?'

'Yes. It was quicker than calling an ambulance.'

'And you stayed.'

He felt the corners of his mouth tug. 'How could I leave you?'

'Thank you.' She found it comforting to think that Theo had watched over her — it made her feel safe. But then she frowned; a memory niggled and she tried to make sense of it.

'He was going to set me up — with a man, Jim. He wanted you to think I was carrying on with him.'

She'd never seen Theo so angry and, for a moment, she wondered whether she should have told him. She watched as he took a deep breath and then forced his clenched fists to relax.

'He's been arrested,' he said shortly. 'You'll have to give a statement later.'

'Did you call the police?'

He nodded. 'And if I hadn't, then the hospital would have. He wasn't even sure what he'd given you — something he'd bought off the internet. He could have killed you. I hope they lock him up for life.'

'But I'm okay, thanks to you.' She smiled at him, feeling warmth as he relaxed and gave an answering grin. She didn't want to upset him again, but she wanted to get the whole sorry incident out in the open so there were no nasty surprises later.

'He was concerned we might not have heard how upset Gina was that you were taking an interest in me on the rebound. She's back and she's ready to fight for her man.'

'I'm not Gina's man. I never was.'

'Not even when you were seeing her?'

'Not even when I was seeing her. She knew the score — that was probably why she slept around behind my back.'

'Oh. I didn't realise. I'm sorry.' She couldn't imagine anyone being unfaithful to Theo — he was so lovely. 'How awful.' She lifted her hand, wanting to make contact, but she stopped just short of his arm.

He shrugged. 'I was annoyed at the time. Now it barely registers. I have other things to occupy me these days.'

Hesitantly — almost shyly — he reached out and took her hand, stroked the back of her fingers with his thumb. 'And my interest in you was never on the rebound.'

'Do you think of yourself as my man?' The words were out before she could stop them, and Theo's gold eyes widened in shock. She immediately regretted asking — she really didn't want to hear the answer. But it only took a nanosecond before he recovered and brought her fingers to be grazed by his lips in an achingly tender gesture.

'Body and soul.' He tucked her hand close to his heart. 'Why didn't you just tell him the truth — that you'd resigned your job and dumped me? By the sounds of it, he'd have left you alone if he'd known. Why put yourself in that danger?'

She leaned back against the starched, white pillows. 'I found I couldn't tell him I'd resigned. And I didn't want to admit that whatever was between us was over.'

He grinned his trademark megawatt grin and, despite her fragile state, her tummy flipped. She lay back, content, and before she knew it had drifted off to sleep again.

★   ★   ★

Theo took her home later that day. Although, she realised, this wasn't really her home. Theo had been wonderful and allowed her to stay and to work here, but she wasn't under any illusions. The house came with the job and, now she'd resigned, she had no rights here at all. She wondered if she should offer to vacate the premises immediately.

She sat back on the sofa in the pretty sitting room, with her feet up and Theo prepared to act on her every whim. Was she too cold? Did she need anything to eat or drink? Really, he was so attentive. And there was no need for him to be.

'I thought I should maybe leave the estate sooner rather than later.' She eventually voiced her thoughts.

'Why would you want to do that? You fought so hard to stay.'

'I no longer work here. Evie's settled with her aunt. And you wanted vacant possession when you arrived, so I feel it's only fair to give you that option now.'

His slashing smile sent ripples down her spine. She couldn't afford to let herself remember she also loved him.

'As I recall, I never did manage to throw you out. You wormed your way into my life and wouldn't budge.'

'Well, I'm suggesting I go now.'

He shook his dark head and eased himself into the chair nearest Rosie's sofa. 'I've employed hordes of work-men, architects, designers to remodel the manor into whatever you want it to be and now you're threatening to bale on me?'

She sighed softly. 'Yes, I know how much you paid those people to drop everything and renovate the manor at short notice. But I'm not going to feel bad about it — you've already told me you're so rich I couldn't make a dent in your fortune.'

She watched his full lips as he smiled and remembered how it had felt to kiss him.

'If you married me, our assets would be shared.'

What? Her heart flipped. But he was joking, he had to be. Theo had told her he didn't do marriage. She replied in the same flippant tone. 'Gee, thanks. Does that offer to share your assets include the manor?'

Theo leaned closer. She could feel his heat, smell his fresh, very male scent. Despite everything, he was doing some very strange things to her equilibrium. 'Nope.'

She laughed. 'Thought not.'

'Because I spoke to my lawyers from your bedside yesterday. I've arranged for the manor and the estate to be transferred into your sole name.' He spoke quietly. Almost as though he were embarrassed by the sentimentality of the occasion.

Rosie's head snapped round. Had she heard correctly?

'The manor's yours,' he repeated, just to clarify matters.

'I don't want it.' She harrumphed ungraciously.

'In that case you're at liberty to sell it,' he told her quietly. 'But I hope you don't. You can make a real go of this place — if you want to.'

'You are joking.'

'I'm deadly serious, Rosie. I'd never joke about an asset of that value.'

She took a moment to digest this. 'Why? Why would you want to hand over the manor and the estate to me?'

'It was to be your wedding present.'

'You don't need to give me a wedding present, we're not getting married. Neither of us believes in marriage.'

'Hear me out, and if you still want to refuse me I'll respect that. But you'll still need somewhere to live — and the estate and everything on it will be yours, regardless.'

'Doesn't that leave a gap in your balance sheet?'

'I've covered that by moving personal funds.'

'Why? You don't need to give me anything. I desperately needed a home for Evie, it's true, but even at that point I'd never have married you for the estate. It was never about your money — I thought you knew that.'

'Will you stop being so stubborn for a minute?' He reached out and gently brushed a red curl from her cheek. 'When I first saw the manor, my instinct was to ditch it as quickly as possible. I was horrified Lysander had bought it in the name of Bradley's.'

'I remember the day I showed you around. I thought you were going to have a fit . . . '

'I was horrified, but as soon as I saw you, I didn't want to get rid of the manor. I wanted to keep it for you. I'm having it renovated for you. And I still very much hope we can make the estate our family home — in this house, if you still prefer. My company can rent the manor from you — I'm looking to move my headquarters out of London.'

She looked at him uncomprehendingly. 'A family home — as in for you, me and babies?'

'Yes.'

She thought through the implications. He was offering her almost everything she'd wanted since she realised she was in love with him. But the one missing ingredient preyed on her mind. Could she love him enough for two?

'I very much hope you'll agree to marry me and allow me to live here with you. But I'm not taking anything for granted — it's purely your decision.'

'I don't understand why you won't let this go. You could find someone else. You've only settled for me because you wanted a relationship with no strings, no dramas, no demands . . . '

He laughed with genuine warmth, his eyes crinkling, his teeth flashing white. 'You must be joking. I've had more strings and more dramas from you than from every other woman I've ever known put together.'

Rosie's face burned.

'And I wouldn't have it any other way.' He reached out and brushed her cheek with his finger. 'I love the way you blush.' He traced the curve of her face and she leaned into his hand. 'Being with you at the hospital last night gave me a lot of time to think. The conclusion I reached is that I want to be with you more than anything else in the world. Do you think you could manage to give me a chance to get things right?'

'Are you saying all this because it was your brother who put me in hospital? Are you suffering some sort of misplaced guilt?'

'I was already on my way back to you yesterday when Harry phoned. If it wasn't for Lysander, we'd have had this conversation a day sooner. I need to know — could you be happy living here with me?'

'And you'd be happy to move from London? It would work? With all the people you have to meet?'

'I'd be very happy. And I can be in the city quickly if I need to be — I have the helicopter.'

Rosie suppressed a smile at this. 'Yes, I know how much you love your helicopter.'

He ignored her teasing and powered on. 'Although I'm hoping to take a back seat for a few years, take time out to be a husband and father . . . if you'll have me.'

He was serious. Rosie took a deep breath. She could do this. Maybe he would never admit he loved her, but what he was describing sounded very much like love to Rosie. It took great strength not to throw herself flat at him.

'Of course I'll have you. Did you ever doubt it?'

'Truthfully? Yes. You were never that keen on me, even when you were desperate for stability for Evie — and her donkeys.'

'I've been keen all along.' She laughed awkwardly. It felt strange to admit that. 'Right from the minute you turned up and started throwing your weight around.'

He grinned softly and leaned in for a slow, delicious kiss, leaving her in no doubt of his sincerity. 'The only thing that gave me hope,' he murmured huskily, 'was that you seemed to appreciate the attraction between us. The first time we kissed, I began to hope perhaps you found me as irresistible as I found you. But you've been pushing me away ever since.'

'I'd never believed I could feel that

for anyone and it scared me. But it scared me more when I thought I'd lost you.'

He pulled her closer. 'I would have found a way to make you want to marry me . . . However much you protested it wasn't what you wanted.'

'Fear does funny things to people.' Deep breath. She had to tell him now, she couldn't live her life trying to hide it. 'I was frightened because somewhere along the line I fell in love with you, and I knew you didn't want that.'

She looked into his liquid gold eyes and could feel her heart beating against her ribs. The silence seemed to span an age.

He sighed. 'I want that,' he admitted quietly. 'Because somewhere along the line I fell in love with you, too.'

Her eyes widened in amazement. 'You don't believe in love.'

'I've changed my mind. I didn't realise it had happened at first, but from the time a tiny, furious redhead threw me off my own land, I've thought of nothing but you. All I want is to be with you, to hold you in my arms, to make you happy. If that's not love then I don't know what is.'

She lifted her arms around his neck and kissed him deeply. They were both breathless when she eventually pulled away.

'So, Rosie Farnham, I love you utterly and completely. Will you marry me?'

She kept him waiting for just a moment while her heart regained a steadier rhythm.

'Yes, Theo Bradley, I will.'

THE END

We do hope that you have enjoyed reading this large print book.

Did you know that all of our titles are available for purchase?

We publish a wide range of high quality large print books including:
**Romances, Mysteries, Classics
General Fiction
Non Fiction and Westerns**

Special interest titles available in large print are:
**The Little Oxford Dictionary
Music Book, Song Book
Hymn Book, Service Book**

Also available from us courtesy of Oxford University Press:
**Young Readers' Dictionary
(large print edition)
Young Readers' Thesaurus
(large print edition)**

For further information or a free brochure, please contact us at:
**Ulverscroft Large Print Books Ltd.,
The Green, Bradgate Road, Anstey,
Leicester, LE7 7FU, England.
Tel:** (00 44) **0116 236 4325
Fax:** (00 44) **0116 234 0205**

DESTINY CALLING

Chrissie Loveday

It is 1952. William Cobridge has returned from a trip to America a different man. Used to a life of luxury, he had been sent away to learn about life in the real world. He meets teacher Paula Frost on a visit to see her aunt, the housekeeper at Cobridge House. He is keen to see Paula again and asks her for a date. Could this be the start of a new romance? But then, things never go smoothly . . .

WHERE I BELONG

Helen Taylor

When a mysterious Italian man arrives on the doorstep in a storm, Maria can hardly turn him away, even though the guesthouse is closed for the winter. Maria's gentle care helps Dino recover from his distressing news, and soon she risks losing her heart to this charismatic stranger. But he has commitments that will take him far away, and her future is at the guesthouse. Can two people from different walks of life find a way to be together?

WED FOR A WAGER

Fenella Miller

Grace Hadley must enter into a marriage of convenience with handsome young Rupert Shalford, otherwise Sir John, her step-father, will sell her to the highest bidder. But Rupert's older brother Lord Ralph Shalford has other ideas and is determined he will have the union dissolved. However, Sir John is equally determined to recover his now missing step-daughter. Will Grace ever find the happiness she deserves?

OUR DAY WILL COME

Sally Quilford

When handsome American airman Ben Greenwood walks into the Quiet Woman pub, the landlord's pretty daughter Betty Yeardley is immediately attracted to him. But Betty is promised to Eddie Simpson, who has been missing in action for two years. With a stocking thief putting the villagers of Midchester on edge, and Eddie's parents putting pressure on Betty to keep her promise, she is forced to fight her growing feelings for Ben.

LOVE'S MASQUERADE

Phyllis Mallett

Cassie Overton, sales director of her father's company, meets Alex Mayfield when he comes on business to strike a deal and they hit it off. Then Cassie is delighted to accept Alex's offer of a holiday, accompanying him back to his affluent family home in Tarango in the West Indies. Once there however, Cassie is compelled to comply with Alex's duplicity in fooling his grandfather and his brother Adam that she's his fiancée . . . then finds it's Adam that she loves.